PRAISE

"A gem of a novel."
THE WISHING SHELF

"A touching, deceptively deep novel for anyone who ever loved."
BOOKMUSE

"Icasia is one of those beautifully crafted characters that we can
see the best of ourselves in."
MONKEY REVIEW

"I have not been so comforted by a novel for a long time."
K. PARSEY, WRITER

"A quick, delicious and important read... that is, if you are
constantly wondering what this life here is for."
ELAINA BATTISTA-PARSONS, AUTHOR OF ITALIAN BONES IN THE SNOW

"Wow. A book I will be thinking about for a while to come."
PERRY ILES, EDITOR

"A metaphor for our times, lives and society, and shows what we
should strive to achieve."
PETER SNELL, BOOKSELLER

"This novel is indeed a rare bird."
JEAN GILL, AUTHOR OF THE NATURAL FORCES SERIES

"Totally absorbing race against time."
STEVE ZETTLER, AUTHOR OF CARELESS LOVE

About the Author

Jessica Bell is an award-winning author/poet, writing/publishing coach, graphic designer, and singer-songwriter who was born in Melbourne, Australia.

In addition to having published a memoir, five novels, three poetry collections, and her bestselling *Writing in a Nutshell* series, she has been featured in a variety of publications and ABC Radio National shows such as *Writer's Digest, Publisher's Weekly, The Guardian, Life Matters,* and *Poetica.*

For more information about Jessica and her projects, visit, *iamjessicabell.com.*

HOW ICASIA BLOOM TOUCHED HAPPINESS

jessica bell

vineleavespress.com

How Icasia Bloom Touched Happiness
Copyright © 2021 Jessica Bell

All rights reserved.
Print Edition
ISBN: 978-1-925965-60-5
Published by Vine Leaves Press 2021

This is a work of fiction. Any similarity between the characters and situations within its pages and places or persons, living or dead, is unintentional and coincidental.

Cover design by Jessica Bell
Cover and interior images by ayaankabir, Thomas, Richard Seeley, Sima
Interior design by Amie McCracken

A catalogue record for this book is available from the National Library of Australia

To all who seek the bluebird.

LISTEN

DeathCare therapists used to say, "Die happy, live happier." It was plastered on billboards, on the sides of buses, on the napkins at McCrackador's, and in at least two ads in every inTel Comm-Brk. The therapists would show their pearly whites and recite it like a star in a buy-this-toothpaste-coaxing.

Die happy. Live happier.

I guess we were brainwashed. I'll let you be the judge of that, Eve. Looks to me like you are already disgusted, not that I blame you.

I have to admit, though, the sentiment was fine. But during compulsory therapy sessions—which were free to every law-abiding citizen in their First Life Phase—they made us believe that in order to die happy, we had to have successful and fulfilling careers. So that's what most people did. They chose a profession and aimed to be the best at it.

I didn't. In all honesty, I also chose not to work or live with my son's sperm donor because I thought it would give me the opportunity to spend quality time with Abel, making sure *he* would die happy instead of me. I had no dream of becoming anyone. I learned too late.

So I lived by swapping favors. That's why homeless stats were down to pretty much zero. Tit-for-tat, that was the official term.

I accepted my life as a tatter. Without a job or a successful career, I knew I would not 'die happy,' but I couldn't expect my son to take responsibility for my future. I would not move onto the Second Life Phase.

I figured I'd do my best to give Abel that chance. And that was good enough for me.

Until I met the Beyetts.

Make yourself comfortable, Eve. You've got a lot to learn before we begin.

Selma Beyett had opened a bakery a few blocks from my squat. I'd been eyeing it for a couple weeks while under construction. As soon as the shop window was painted with *Selma's Sweets & Savories*, I knew it would be the place where I could score me and Abel a daily breakfast deal, and maybe a loaf of bread for lunch.

I was good at selling food. Everybody needs food. So I figured in exchange for some goods, I could start bringing clientele to Selma's shop.

But it didn't quite work out that way.

When I opened the door, the aroma of baked bread, chocolate cake, and mint slice filled my senses. It was a smell I'd daydreamed about but never actually experienced, so I stood there, breathing deeply, in and out, as the door chimed closed, thinking how much nicer this bakery was compared to the ones I'd seen in the *When Today Was Then* show. Having never set foot out of my own neighborhood, the only bread and sweets I saw were mass produced and sold in plastic. And scoring a tit-for-tat in a mainstream Sparket was like asking for a stone to donate blood.

Selma rubbed her hands dry on a red and white striped tea towel and smiled. Her curly bright orange hair was held out of her face by a thick black headband. She wore black, head to toe, leggings and turtleneck. No jewelry, no make-up.

I felt self-conscious about my scraggly and limp mousy-brown Mohawk and 50-year-old brown leather jacket that was cracked around the shoulders and cuffs. What made me feel like a cool kid on the streets made me feel like a pauper in Selma's presence.

"Hello there," Selma said. Her tone wasn't high or low, but captured the same kindness you hear in your favorite schoolteacher's voice. "You're my first customer. Do you think that might be lucky?"

I walked toward the counter with my hand held out in confidence.

"Hi. I have a proposal for you," I said. I figured I'd just get right to it. Experience had taught me that the more fore-play you engage in, the more focus you begin to lose on the main event. I once walked out of a shop with a good working knowledge of bioengineering, but no food.

"Oh," Selma nodded. "Would you like to try one of my peach danishes first?"

I blushed. Here was this lovely lady standing before me, offering me food before I'd even asked for any, and all I wanted to do was make the deal and get a move on. She must have noticed my cheeks turn red because she added, "On me, of course."

I was speechless. Free? For no exchange? That was unheard of in those days, Eve.

Selma slipped a freshly baked danish onto a napkin and handed it to me. I took it, sniffed it, closed my eyes to make sure what I was smelling was as delicious as it looked. With my eyes still closed, I took a bite. Saliva flooded the sides of my mouth and I groaned in pleasure.

Selma chuckled. I opened my eyes.

"Oh shit," I said, wiping my mouth on my sleeve. "I'm so rude. My name's Icasia Bloom. This danish is the most delicious thing I have ever eaten in my whole goddamn life."

It was Selma's turn to blush.

She wiped her hand on her thigh, and it left a faint white handprint of flour. She held it out for me to shake.

"I'm Selma. Just Selma will do." She nodded at her shop front window. "As you are probably already aware." We shook hands. "Please, take a seat," she said, gesturing behind me.

I turned around and saw that she only had one table and two chairs. I looked at her questioningly. Maybe I could try and wrangle her some furniture in exchange for some food, I thought. But before I could say anything, she beat me to it.

"I believe that less sitting space means there's less chance of people hanging around for hours, making one coffee and a muffin last all day."

I nodded. Smart, I thought. Maybe this wasn't going to be as easy a deal as I'd expected. I'd always thrived on making deals with newbie businesses. They were afraid of failing and welcomed the assistance.

"Oh, dear me, please forgive me, I didn't offer you a coffee!" Selma stood up, but I grabbed her hand and said, "Dude, I'm fine. Really."

She stared at the tattoo of the Sanskrit swastika on the inside of my wrist. She paused, halfway out of her seat.

I stopped chewing. I had a feeling that my gesture had backfired. Anger glistened in her eyes. Or was it concern? Had she regretted asking me to sit down? Maybe she didn't know that the swastika was originally a symbol of life, strength and good luck. I was not one of those Nazis from back in the day when the Globe was separated into countries, when leaders in various governments played Russian Roulette with cryptocurrency and sent the world tumbling into the greatest depression in its entire history, but I panicked that she thought I was, so I pulled my hand away, grabbed my bag and said, "I'm really sorry to have bothered you. Thanks so much for the danish. I'll be sure to recommend this place to anyone I can." I stood up quickly to leave.

I was kicking myself. I'd done it again. Got sidetracked by the pleasantries and neglected the real purpose of my visit.

Selma sat in silence as I walked to the door. I paused for a moment, thinking I should stop being so embarrassed and presumptuous and ask her for a deal anyway. But for some reason I couldn't. I opened the door, but as it chimed, I heard the sound of a chair scraping along the floor.

"You said you had a proposal for me."

I released the handle and let the door swing shut.

It chimed again, and I swiveled around, forcing a smile that made me feel like a con-artist. I took a deep breath, trying to rid myself of the confident facade—my survival tactic—and be as genuine as possible.

"Yeah." I said. "I do."

Selma held out an upturned hand toward the chair opposite her. "Please. Sit. Tell me."

I sat down, hugging my backpack to my chest, staring at my half-eaten danish on the table. My mouth watered. I really wanted to finish it.

"I was wondering if you'd be interested in a tit-for-tat," I said. "For a few food items every day, I would bring you clientele, and continue to do so until you wished to terminate the agreement." I tried to be as articulate as possible. I wasn't really used to it, but Selma seemed so articulate herself, I thought she might see me as a dumb aimless juvenile if I didn't. You might think that's hard to imagine looking at me now, but trust me when I say that despite being self-educated in PreGlobe culture and history, being street smart when I needed to be, and making the best of whatever was available, one vital element I lacked in life was social etiquette. That was a lesson I should have learned from birth, not at fifteen when I was expected to move out of my home and have a child. Not when I was hit all of a sudden with adult responsibilities and a completely new way of life.

Eve, I know. You look confused. You probably have more questions. But I'll answer those later.

Back to me asking for a tit-for-tat.

Selma nodded and flattened her hands on the table in front of her.

"A *few* items of food?" she asked.

"Yeah. I have a son," I said, in case she thought I was asking for too much. "He's five."

Selma nodded the same way again, staring down at her hands as if this information had no impact on her decision process at all.

She didn't move or say a word for ages. I could hear the air travel through my nose it was so quiet. I thought maybe she had slipped into a meditative state.

"I can give you a loaf of bread every day. And two pastries." She hesitated. "And a liter of freshly squeezed juice. But you can't be fussy about the juice because I can only get what's at the Sparket that day." She paused and stared at me in a way that suggested she was trying to size me up. "I don't shop at the Underground during the week. There are always WarDens fining people."

"Wise." I said it a little too loudly, and cleared my throat. "I can guarantee you at least one new customer per day. Would that be sufficient?"

Selma shook her head. "No. No. Not at all."

I was taken by surprise. No? I didn't know if I could get her more than one new customer a day. I had never managed that kind of consistency before. And if I didn't keep it consistent, would she renege? It's happened to me before and I was left scavenging food off my stingy neighbor for over two weeks.

"Uh ... I," I stammered, not sure if I should risk it. I didn't want to fail her. But I didn't want to fail Abel even more. If she was going to refuse me food on the days when I didn't bring anyone in, I'd—

Then the most unexpected thing happened.

Selma reached out to me, took my hands, and turned them over so that my palms were facing upward.

She stared at my tattoos. Motionless. On my other wrist, I had the Four Blessings symbol.

"I don't need customers," she said, after a few moments had passed. She looked up, and a tear slid down her cheek. "I just need someone to talk to."

I swallowed. That tear spoke of a hardship I knew absolutely nothing about. This woman seemed to have it all. But I was basing my opinion merely on her appearance and her way of speaking. Maybe she was like me. Maybe all this was just a front to get by.

So I just nodded.

At that moment in time, Eve, it seemed the only appropriate thing to do, don't you think?

WATCH

Despite the fresh glow on Selma's face the next morning, it looked as if she had slept the night at the bakery. She wore the same outfit as the day before and still sported the floury fingerprints on her behind.

Icasia hovered by the door as she removed her jacket, waiting for Selma to take it and hang it over a chair.

"Good morning. How are you today?" Instead of taking Icasia's jacket, Selma handed her a rucksack full of Jacobson coffee, Twindlings Tea, and Burycad hot chocolate for Abel. A few glass bottles of fresh juice, whole fresh fruits and vegetables from the Underground (she'd risked it after all), and even scraps of dough wrapped in baking paper. There was so much produce that any bystander would have interpreted it as back payment for a week's worth of successful tatting.

Icasia opened the rucksack and stood with her mouth agape.

"Too much, too fast?" Selma said with a nervous chuckle.

"Dude … I … er…" Icasia shook her head.

"I'm sorry. I look like a desperate girlfriend now, don't I?"

Icasia put her jacket into the rucksack and zipped it shut with a smile.

"Of course you don't. Thank you. This is, uh, generous."

Selma returned to the counter and sieved cinnamon over

a tray of custard tarts to hide the hot embarrassment that made her cheeks visibly pulse. She placed a few tarts inside the glass cabinet, and took the rest out back, bar one. On her return, she held the tart out for Icasia, who took it with an uneasy smile after resting the heavy rucksack by the front door.

Selma disappeared again and returned with two mugs of steaming coffee with Polaroid type photos on the sides of them. One showed a grown man wearing sunglasses, and the other a young blonde girl. She placed them on the table, sighed, rubbed her hands together and sat down. Icasia stared in wonderment as Selma grabbed the remote control, switched on the inTel, and turned the volume down to zero.

Icasia smiled at the way the inTel protruded from the wall in a silver casing that looked like the front of an oven as she waited for Selma to ask her to sit down too. She didn't. Instead, she stared at the muted *Morning Globe Show*, nodding in agreement to things no-one could hear. Icasia placed her custard tart by the other mug of coffee on the table and sat down without invitation. She cleared her throat.

"I was wondering how long you were just going to stand there." Selma patted Icasia's arm without looking at her. "Didn't peg you as the easily intimidated type."

The corner of Icasia's mouth twitched as she grinned. Selma slurped her coffee, and turned to look her in the eye. "Conversations don't start themselves, you know."

Icasia took a deep breath, nodded, and opened her mouth to speak. But nothing came out.

"Uh—" Icasia took another bite of her tart and spoke with her mouth full, "Do you like custard tarts?" Her cheeks turned bright red.

Selma chuckled and stroked Icasia's cheek, and Icasia jerked her head back with a look of horror on her face.

Selma pulled her hand back quickly. "Oh my goodness, I'm so sorry. You reminded me of my daughter, and I had already touched you before I realized what I was doing." Selma cupped her own cheeks and shook her head. "That was foolish. I apologize. Could we ... perhaps, start over?" It was a huge relief to both women that they had made slight fools of themselves.

"Yeah. Let's do that," Icasia chuckled.

"So, tell me about your son. Abel, was it?"

"Yeah. He's five. He's just started school, at the one around the corner from here—"

"Oh, my daughter goes to Jacobson Smith Birchford Wagner Brown K-8, too."

Icasia laughed. "Glad one of us remembers its name."

"It's ridiculous, isn't it?"

"Yeah. Any idea why the name is so long?"

"I've heard it's got something to do with Governor Jacobson's family heritage."

"Yeah, about that. Is it just me, or does he seem like a bit of a wanker?" Icasia gritted her teeth.

"A what?"

"An asshat."

"Ah. He is a bit of a..." Selma hesitated, "dingbat, isn't he? His voice reminds me of a gremlin."

Icasia nodded, not knowing what a gremlin was. She's heard the word but can't put an image to it. She should have known, especially given her recent obsession with hanging in the history aisle at the library.

"How old is your daughter?" Icasia said after a long pause.

"Leila's just turned thirteen."

"Oh," Icasia whispered. Silence. She turned to the inTel and held the news anchor's gaze until the break between reports. "You've still got two years to sort that out."

Selma breathed in and out and rubbed her lips together. "We do. But I'd rather not drag the process out. She knows it's coming. The knowing is hard enough to deal with. I'm not sure I should keep her hanging onto that uncertainty. I'd rather we just rip the plaster right off and get on with it."

"I get that. Your husband is supportive, right?"

Selma raised her eyebrows.

"Uh, sorry, if you have a husband."

"It's okay. I do. His name's Jerome. But he wasn't an assigned donor. We got married five years ago, and he and Leila don't have a very good relationship. I suppose there are always pros and cons to disobeying the Book."

"You can say that again. But I'd much rather keep my independence."

"What independence?" Selma smiled.

Both women returned their attention to the inTel and sipped their coffees.

After a long pause, Icasia said, "Sorry about Leila."

"It's fine. I'm used to taking responsibility for her, though it can get a bit expensive when she's sick. But Jerome's the love of my life. I wouldn't change a thing."

The corner of Icasia's mouth twitched slightly. "Have you booked an appointment at Prems?" she asked.

"I have," Selma said, running her middle finger along the rim of her coffee cup. "But I haven't told Leila yet. I'm dreading that, to be honest."

A few moments passed before Selma's eyes suddenly lit up. "Maybe ... maybe you could—" Selma snorted and waved a hand in dismissal. "No, that's probably silly. Don't worry about it."

Icasia's stomach rumbled.

"Brking News" started flashing on the inTel. It caught

Selma's attention as she downed the last of her coffee. She grabbed the remote control, swallowed quickly, and turned up the volume.

It has officially been announced by Governor Jacobson today that the temporary overload problems regarding our Transition Graves has now become a permanent threat. Unfortunately, the growth of individuals between the First and Second Life Phase is nearing its limit due to a growing number of life goals not being met.

Governor Jacobson states that in order to avoid the ever-increasing overload causing fatal glitches in spiritual data within the Transition Graves, a new course of action will be effective immediately.

Governor Jacobson assures us that the same rules to the Transition Graves will apply: Transitioners will be released into the Second Life Phase as soon as their legal offspring meet their life goals. There will, however, be a set time limit for meeting life goals from this point forward.

The new law states that if an individual's goal has not yet been met by the age of 39.5, they will be required to participate in DeathCare Therapy to help them reach their desired goal. If that desired goal has not been met within six months of the start of DeathCare Therapy sessions, death will be induced at 40.0 years of age, instead of the current 60.0. However, unlike those who are death-induced at 60.0 years of age, new recipients of DeathCare Therapy will not be held in a Transition Grave, and will not have the chance to move onto the Second Life Phase when their legal offspring successfully meet their goal. Instead, their souls shall be immediately annihilated to make room for individuals who have qualified for transition.

Governor Jacobson firmly states, however, that we have nothing at all to fear as long as we "put our best foot forward." He also adds that individuals already over the age of 40.0 will not be affected by this new law.

The news report was followed by an ad for DeathCare Therapy. Stringed music accompanied by images of people being hooked up to death-inducement thrones, with their children laughing, clapping and clinking champagne glasses as their parents faded out. At the end, a male and a female therapist said with toothy grins, "Put your best foot forward today and make your parents proud. Die happy, live happier."

Icasia rolled her eyes, coughed "Bullshit" and took another bite of her tart. Selma's face drained completely of color, and she burst into tears. She grabbed Icasia's hand and shook it.

"Jerome is 39.5, and he has not yet met his goal." She breathed in and out, her exhale jagged, like the air was catching in her throat. She swiped the tears from her cheeks. "His father is almost 60.0, and his mother's in a Transition Grave. We *have* to do something. I can't watch him fail his parents. I... I can't watch the love of my life be put down like a sick dog."

The word "we" echoed throughout the room.

And now there was no turning back.

LISTEN

I had never heard a stranger use the word "we" before in relation to something that involved me. And to be honest, Eve, the word "love" made me feel a little ill. Oh come on, Eve, why such an expression of shock? Can you blame me? I'd never been in love before. I loved Abel, but that didn't count. That was a different kind of love, I was pretty certain of it. It wasn't the type of love that led to sex. I'd read about sex. I'd even been on the Sex Simulator after my previous gynecological check-up to see what it felt like.

You must have so many questions. Let me explain something quickly before we get back to Selma and the bakery.

It was illegal for women to have sex until they'd had their donor child. And if you ever became naturally impregnated by your lover's sperm, the law demanded a termination. Most women just had their tubes tied after having their donor baby to avoid the hassle. I'd never known anything different, so it didn't really bother me. But I'd read in the history books about women who had already had sex before the Jacobson Movement. They fought to try and make natural birth legal again. All the protesters were put down— bar a small handful who succumbed and promised to obey the rules—and their souls were annihilated. The protests stopped pretty quickly after that.

For men it was different. They were taught to accept whatever the female wanted. They were required to donate their sperm to PremsBank. And once a donor's sperm was assigned to a female, the female had the choice to marry the donor or marry another single donor—regardless of whether they had been inseminated with their sperm or not—and raise the child with him. If the female didn't want to, that was fine, too. But it was encouraged by the incentive of free health care for the entire family during their FLP, so most women took advantage of it.

I guessed that Selma, like me, hadn't taken that option.

I was getting to like Selma a lot. And believe me, Eve, I didn't find it easy to like people. You couldn't trust anybody then. Especially when it came to getting free stuff. I was used to using people. I didn't often care about anyone except me and Abel. But this experience was *making* me care. And the feeling was ... soothing.

As the news of the new law broke, I thought about my parents, who had already accepted annihilation as there was no one in the Second Life Phase they particularly wanted to see. If they weren't going to transition, then I didn't feel like I had any reason to either. And Abel had plenty of time to sort himself out. He was only five, and I wasn't going to be a burden on him. What use would he have had for a direction-less mother in the Second Life Phase anyway? I had taught him not to hold onto family as religiously as the Jacobson Movement preached. "Family is not everything," I'd say to him. "The world is what *you* make it, not what *they* make it." I'd told him that in the long run, the only thing that mattered was taking care of himself and doing what made him happy in the now.

But. Jerome's fate made me wonder what it truly felt like to care so passionately about dying happy and living happier, rather than just surviving. I was now a lot more than just curious about Selma. Her predicament had started to affect my general outlook on life.

As the tears streamed down Selma's cheeks, a remnant of longing pinched at my heart. I had promised myself not to get mixed up in other people's messes so that I could concentrate on Abel. But there was something about Selma and the kindness she had shown me that made me want to help her. I was also beginning to realize that with Selma's family situation, she mightn't have had many friends, if any. So we had something in common. The conserve types tended to turn their noses up at women who didn't marry a single donor. And most people were conserves.

I wiped a tear from under Selma's left eye with my thumb, somewhat hesitantly.

"It's okay. We'll figure something out," I said. "I promise."

Eve, I had *no* idea what I was promising. But it was no longer just me and Abel and my parents.

Three days passed as I prowled the neighborhood for bakery customers. Every time I stopped by, Selma was in tears and we hardly talked. She gave me food and shadows and shyness.

By day four, she was able to talk about meaningful day-to-day activities, like how many weevils she'd picked from the flour. One by one. For ten hours straight.

By day five, I'd gotten her five clients. One per day. I was satisfied with that, but it was an accident. They looked like they'd been looking at too many Jacobson Movement advertising archives. They wore blue vintage skirt suits and tied their hair back. They had no make-up, no jewelry, no style. All of them were women, and all of them lived by the Book.

I lied and told them Selma was too.

Selma said, "Thank you. You didn't have to do that," out of the blue one day when I was helping her put icing on cupcakes.

I knew she wasn't thanking me for the cupcakes.

When I walked into the bakery a full week after the Brking News report, same time as usual, Selma was already sitting at the table with two coffees and two slices of carrot cake with cream cheese frosting. I tell you, Eve, I was *thoroughly* enjoying those sweets. I'd been deprived of sugar for years, as I couldn't be fussy over what I was given as a tatter.

Selma didn't look at me. She didn't smile. She didn't even say hello. I had expected another day like the previous five. Hardly talking, just being there. Sitting. Listening to each other breathe.

Selma sniffed, pinched off a chunk of carrot cake with her fingers, squashed it and stuffed it into her mouth.

"Do you remember at school," she mumbled, "how they taught us that leading a life by the Book would bring peace, happiness, and success?"

I didn't. I never paid attention in Jacobson Studies. My parents had always said that the novelty would soon wear off. That the world was just going through a phase. I nodded anyway.

"Well, I always dismissed the idea," Selma said. I thought that no matter how I chose to live my life, I would make the most of it, and that happiness was in the eye of the beholder."

I sat down and sipped my coffee. It was cold. She must have been waiting for me to arrive for ages. She hadn't touched her coffee either. Was she just staring at the muted inTel again and waiting for me? Everything seemed to be prepared in the shop. Clean, tidy, that mouth-wateringly sweet smell. But the table was covered in crumbs and dried coffee splashes. I wondered why she hadn't bothered wiping it down.

I waited a moment to see if Selma would continue her thoughts, and watched a few tears splash on her hand. I rummaged in my backpack for a tissue. The only one I could find was crinkled and used. I decided against giving it to her and wiped her hand and face dry with my palm pushed into my sleeve.

"Does this have anything to do with that announcement?" I asked in a near-whisper, not sure whether it was appropriate to bring it up since she had avoided the topic until now. But what I really wanted to ask was, *who are you?*

Selma held two fingers to my wrist. I could see her counting in her head—eyes closed, lips barely moving. "Fifty beats. Do you run?"

I had no idea what the significance was, but I played along. Something was churning around her head and I didn't want to interrupt her train of thought.

"No, but I walk. A lot."

Selma nodded. "Good. That's very good."

I squinted in question.

"I'm not insane. I'm—" Selma picked at a thread coming loose at the cuff of my leather jacket and something in me snapped.

I flicked her hand away. "Dude, I worked hard for this. Don't ruin it."

"I can sew it back."

"But you won't need to if you don't pull it out."

"It's coming loose anyway."

"If it comes completely loose, you'll be the first to know."

What was this? I thought. We sounded like bickering spouses. We stared at each other in silence until I glanced at the clock.

"Please don't go yet." Selma breathed in so deeply I swear I could hear her bronchioles stretch.

"Why?"

"I need you."

"But I'm not doing anything but sitting here."

"Would you like to not just sit here?"

I tensed up. I sensed a big question coming, Eve.

Selma did ask me a big question. But not until after she'd recounted the events of the previous week.

WATCH

During dinner on the night of the new legislation announcement, Selma suggested Leila join her and Jerome on the couch to watch the premiere of *50 Shades of Childbirth*, a new docudrama inTel series about PremsBank and the lives of a few young women.

Leila shook her head and looked into her lap.

"Come on, honey, I need you to understand what it's going to be like there. It was so long ago since I was there myself, and I worry I won't be able to offer you the right information."

"I don't want any information," Leila snapped, flicking her long brown frizzy fringe out of her face.

"But who is going to give it to you, if not me? Are they preparing you at school for this?"

Leila shook her head again. Her bottom lip trembled as she touched her stomach.

Jerome downed his half-full glass of red wine and cleared his throat. "What have I said about looking your mother in the eye when she's talking to you, Leila?"

Leila gritted her teeth and glared at him. "You said nothing about it except that I should, and I told you I would look anywhere I wanted."

"Right." Jerome tapped his forefinger on the table next to his plate. "That back-talk calls for—"

"No." Selma, interrupted him and rested her hand on his arm. His muscles were clenched, but they relaxed under Selma's touch. "Stop this. Both of you. You are both under incredible stress right now, and I think we should all support each other in this time of great change instead of making it worse by being selfish with our emotions."

"Oh, *stop* trying to reconcile everything, Selma. Emotions are emotions. Just let them be. Let them come out." Jerome stomped his foot and accidently banged his knee on the underside of the table. "Dammit." He winced. "And don't even try to begin to think you understand anything about what I'm going through. My hands have not stopped shaking since this morning." He held them above his plate. Selma and Leila glanced at them.

"Of course I understand." Selma frowned. Leila rolled her eyes and scoffed.

"Perhaps you don't understand that I may very well lose the love of my life in six months' time, and there is nothing I can do about it," Selma said, half-directing her words at Leila. "This is worse than you being terminally ill, Jerome." Selma lowered the volume in her voice and squeezed Jerome's knee under the table. "There is no treatment that leads to a definite cure. How helpless do you think that makes me feel? And what about the trauma that Leila is about to go through? Do you understand how hard it is to become a mother when you are still a child? That's something I can definitely understand, and I don't intend to let Leila go through it on her own."

"I can look after myself." Leila crossed her arms and flung herself into the backrest with a smack.

Silence.

"No," Jerome said quietly. "No, you can't." He reached out to hold Leila's arm, but she snatched it away and ground her teeth.

"Since when have you ever cared about me, Dad? You think we have something in common now? That because we're both trapped by the stupid system I'll finally love you? Go eat dirt."

Leila stood up and ran out of the room. Jerome made a movement to follow, scraping his chair along the ceramic tiles, but Selma shook her head and gestured for Jerome to sit back down.

"Just let her go, Jome. I'll talk to her in private about Prems before we go to bed." Selma rubbed her brow and sighed.

"When is she going to accept me? What am I doing wrong?" Jerome ran his hands through his floppy dark brown hair.

"You're not doing anything wrong. She got used to it being just me and her, that's all. You know that. She'll get over it when she grows up."

"I doubt it."

"I think you should be focusing on yourself. Forget about Leila for now. It's not going to do you any good."

Jerome sighed and pinched the bridge of his nose. "Let's take a breather in the loungeroom."

On the couch, Jerome rested his elbows on his knees and his head in his palms. His shoulders shook, and it took a few moments for Selma to realize he wasn't laughing. He was sobbing. She wrapped her arms around him from the side, resting her chin on his left shoulder, her forehead against his cheek.

"We'll figure something out. Together. I promise."

Jerome nodded and kissed Selma on the head. He sniffed her hair.

"Love you to death, Sma."

Selma knelt down and rested her head sideways in his lap. Jerome stroked her hair with a nostalgic smile. He patted

Selma on the back when her hand started to wander up to his crotch. "We should discuss our options."

Selma stood up and rubbed the back of her neck.

"I'll make us a bourbon coffee."

When Selma returned to the lounge, Jerome was lying on the carpet flat on his back, staring at the ceiling. Selma didn't react as she put the coffees on the table.

"Clearly I need to just accept my fate," Jerome said, maintaining his gaze toward the ceiling.

"Jome, your tone worries me. It unsettles me. It's like you're uttering a statement that's untainted with a fatal consequence."

"Well, this is the new normal, isn't it?" Jerome said, turning to face her without changing his expression or his tone.

"Don't be ridiculous. You'll change careers." Selma said with equal calm.

"But I love Robotics."

"Maybe you just think you do because your father did. Maybe you're just following in his footsteps. Maybe it's not your true calling."

"I think you're forgetting something." Jerome squinted at Selma.

"What am I forgetting?"

"I have six months. How am I going to find a new career path, as well as fulfilment from it, in that time?" Jerome looked at the ceiling again, lifted his arms and rested his head on his hands.

"It's not impossible. That's what DeathCare Therapy is for."

"DeathCare Therapy," Jerome scoffed. "It took me ten years of study and work experience to get this job. DCT is all for show. It's false hope, Sma."

"I disagree. Surely it doesn't have to be a career that requires so much expertise."

"I don't have a choice in what my path to happiness is, so how am I supposed to control something like that?"

"You have to at least try. What about your mother? She's been in her Transition Grave for five years. She needs you in order to move into the SLP, you know that."

"She was never too fussed about transitioning."

Selma stared at Jerome with a look of shock on her face.

"You've never mentioned that before. And what about your father? It's all Gary talks about; finally meeting her in SLP," Selma said, her face growing red. "DCT might help you. The least you can do is keep an open mind. If you don't find happiness, he'll never see your mother again—and neither will you, for that matter. Don't you think you owe him at least that much after all he's done for you?"

Selma watched Jerome's Adam's apple move up and down. A tear slid down his temple. He sat up, wiped it away, and smiled.

"He'll forgive me. Mum will forgive me. We've all had a good life here. Who needs eternal bliss?"

Selma picked up her bourbon coffee with a trembling hand and almost spilled it. She cupped the mug in both hands and brought it to her lips, but didn't take a sip.

"So, you're just ... going to give up?" Selma half-whispered into the mug. She took a sip, and swallowed. "To give up on life? On *me*?" She sniffed and leaned her head back to blink away tears of her own.

Jerome stood and gestured for Selma to do so too. She sobbed into his chest.

"I need you, Jome. I love you. Do you not love me like I love you?"

"Of course, I do. How could you think I don't love you?"

"If you do, how can you even conceive of giving up on me?"

"I'm not giving up on you, Sma. Life has given up on me."

After a couple of hours of sitting silently in front of the inTel sipping slowly on bourbon coffees and sorrow, Jerome went to bed in his study, saying that it would be good practice for Selma to sleep alone. She didn't object. She didn't say a word until Jerome closed the door in her face.

"Well, that might be the coldest thing you have ever done," she whispered to herself.

Selma walked half-way down the corridor, wiping away her tears, and paused in front of Leila's bedroom door. She ran her hands over her thighs and straightened her top before tapping on the door.

"What?"

"It's me."

Leila responded with an 'okay-come-in' grunt. Selma sat on the edge of Leila's bed and squeezed one of Leila's legs over the duvet. Leila poked out the one Mini Amp still plugging her left ear. An incessant industrial thumping buzzed through the tiny speakers until she pressed a button on her bright purple Comm.

"You shouldn't be so hard on your dad. He loves you, you know," Selma said in a gentle tone.

"He's not my dad."

The expression on Selma's face turned from concern to anger. She opened her mouth to speak, but ended up holding her breath for a moment instead.

"Look ... can we talk about Prems?" Selma said.

Leila groaned and covered her head with a pillow.

"Please? If not for you, then for me. I'm nervous about my only child leaving home."

Leila yanked at the pillow and flung it off the side of the bed. She sat up. "Every child is an only child, Mum." Leila tsked.

"That's true. But there's only one that I love."

Leila smiled and traced a daisy on the bedspread with her finger. Selma crawled onto the bed and sat next to her, leaning her head against the headboard with a sigh. Leila rested her head on Selma's shoulder.

"Maybe we can start by you telling me what you know," Selma said softly, "and then we can move forward from there."

Leila balled her fists inside her sleeves. "I know that I have to have a kid. That it's the law."

"Right," Selma said with a curt nod. "Do you know why?"

"Something to do with controlling the amount of people in the world?"

"That's right. You're also only allowed to have one. Your tubes will be also be tied so you can't have more."

"I know. We learned about it in Health. But I don't understand why we have to do it now. It doesn't make sense."

"It says in the Jacobson Guide—the Book—that the reason for this is so people aren't prevented from having a fulfilling sexual relationship. You know what sex is, don't you? I guess they taught you that in Health class too?"

Leila nodded and drew her knees to her chest, hugging them with her balled-up fists.

"I don't get why people can't have sex before having a baby."

"Because then the establishment wouldn't be able to control how many children you have. They probably don't write this in your textbook, but not too long before your father was born, Anima Cemetery didn't exist. There were graveyards, and they were filling up fast. This caused a problem, as the world was running out of land space for them, so they invented the technology we know today. I personally believe it had been invented for years, but they were just trying to find the right moment for it to be revealed so as not to cause world chaos. Then we had that huge economic collapse, which supposedly happened by accident when the leaders of the first world recklessly gambled away trillions in cryptocurrency. So, they say. I won't go into the idea that I think this whole thing was engineered to put people into a perpetual state of fear so that we could be manipulated and controlled more easily. Then suddenly, a rich philanthropist saved us all and took control of the world to make it a better place. And we are now the Globe. And we are all supposedly happier people who have the time to care about the more important things in life without having to worry about Sats.

"That still doesn't explain the sex thing."

"Sex leads to pregnancy. Pregnancy leads to babies. When your tubes are tied after you give birth to your donor child, you can then have sex without the risk of getting pregnant. Too many babies equal too many people. If there are too many people then it's more challenging for Governor Jacobson to take care of us all the way he has been." Selma put air-quotes around 'take care of'.

"Okay, I get it. Too many cooks spoil the broth—that kind of thing?"

Selma laughed. "Yeah, I guess. Something like that."

"So, what's so good about sex that we need to have it, anyway?"

Selma scoffs. "Uh ... well ... it's a bit hard to explain, but when you love someone, it's what our human instincts make us want to do. It's a biological need."

"But if I marry a single donor, how do I know I'll love him?"

Selma stroked Leila's hair. "Despite what they probably told you at school, you don't have to marry a single donor. It's not against the law to refuse marriage. It just means that the government won't give you free health care. But you don't need it. We have Sats. You can be a single mother. We'll help you find your own apartment before the baby is born, and we'll be here to support you all the way. Then one day, you'll find a man that you truly love. Someone who makes you happy. Like I did."

Leila looked away and shook her head. "You mean *you* will be around to help me."

Selma traced the same daisy on the duvet that Leila had traced earlier.

"I'll pick you up after school tomorrow to take you to Prems, okay?"

"What? No!" Leila shrieked and threw herself out the bed. She stood there like she was about to launch into a sprint before squatting on the floor and sobbing.

Selma inched to the edge of the bed to try and console Leila, but she flicked her hand away before she'd even touched her.

"I wouldn't make you do anything that wasn't in your best interests, sweetie."

"But my teacher said we had until we were fifteen. I have two more years!"

"It'll be better for you to just get it out of the way. The sooner you do it, the sooner it will be over, and you can get on with your life. There's no point dragging this out. It's a simple procedure, and there's nothing to be afraid of, okay?"

"What about school? And my friends!"

"Most of the girls in your year will be facing the same thing, sweetie. And you can go back after the birth, or choose to take an apprenticeship in a field that interests you. If you like, we can even send you to a preliminary career analysis to help you figure out what you want to do. We'll support whatever decision you make."

Leila burst into tears and threw punches at Selma. Selma tried to calm her down while holding her tightly in her arms, but Leila's flailing arms and vibrant wails overpowered her attempt. Eventually she grabbed Leila's face in both hands and held her head to her chest. She whispered in her ear, "I love you to the moon and back. I would never do anything to hurt you."

The doorbell rang, and Selma helped Leila back into bed, despite her resistance, before answering it.

Standing tall, in a sky-blue suit, was a Jacobson representative. He handed her an envelope, nodded, saluted, and walked away.

Selma opened it recklessly without closing the front door.

Dear Mrs. Selma Beyett,

Congratulations! You have been granted access to a Transition Grave once you reach the age of 40.0, and your parents, Rose and Terrence Martin, have been released into the Second Life Phase where they will live in eternal harmony.

Please let us take the time to remind you that in order for you to be released into the Second Life Phase, your daughter, Ms. Leila Beyett, must successfully find happiness. If you are interested in providing her with a DeathCare therapist in advance, please contact us at the number below and we will be happy to mail you an introductory booklet free of charge.

Bonus! Due to the fact that you have successfully found happiness under the age of 30.0, Governor Jacobson has generously offered to cover Ms. Leila Beyett's PremsBank and childbirth expenses, and 50% of any medical care she may need thereafter. We hope that this comes as welcome news to you, and that you tell your friends and family about the benefits of finding happiness as early as possible.

Thank you for cooperating with the Jacobson Movement. We wish you well in all your endeavors until the day of your death inducement.

Sincerely Yours,
Norone
Chief Executive Officer
Neural Oscillation Registry
www.nor.com

"Jome!" Selma burst into tears and bolted to Jerome's office. She didn't knock, but pushed the door so hard that it ricocheted off the wall and woke Jerome with a start.

"What's going on?" Jerome yawned and rubbed his face with both hands.

Selma handed him the Letter in a shaking hand. "I'm not going there without you, Jome. You cannot give up on me. Promise you won't give up on me."

Jerome swallowed, sat up, and reached for Selma's hand. He pulled her onto the bed and wrapped her in his arms.

"I won't give up on you," he whispered, hugging Selma tight, "for as long as I'm alive."

Selma and Leila stood outside PremsBank, looking up at the grand pillars that framed a fifty-meter-wide glass wall. Prems was sky blue too—inside and out. Just like it was on inTel. The overwhelming atmosphere of serenity it emanated, however, was not something one could gauge from a screen.

Leila smiled and sniffed in the fresh spring air and sunshine—weather conditions which were only present around Prems that day. Everywhere else in the city, it was raining.

A bluebird chirped and hovered in front of Leila, chirped again and winked, gesturing with its beak toward the entrance. Selma and Leila followed as it led them inside.

There was no door, but as they approached the glass, a section of it melted and parted just enough for them to step through. Everything had changed since Selma was last there.

Once inside, a soft sound of trickling water echoed through the lobby as the glass wall mended itself. The bluebird flew toward the domed ceiling and faded away. The mosaic tiling on the floor incorporated every shade of blue one could imagine, but the tread was soft, like walking on grass.

"Welcome Leila, and greetings Mrs. Beyett. We have been expecting you." A barefoot woman, dressed in a skirt suit that was a slightly darker shade of blue than the representative from the previous night, held out her hand for Selma to shake as she approached them. Leila's eyes glazed over. She hugged the woman around the waist, and looked up at her in awe.

"You may refer to me as Norate. It's lovely to meet you. Please follow me." Norate stroked Leila's hair and offered a comforting smile to Selma, whose eyes also then glazed over as she succumbed to Norate's hypnotic power.

Selma took Leila's hand and they followed Norate through a dimly lit tunnel. Selma repeated the woman's name over and over under her breath, as if trying to understand it more deeply.

Norate, Norate, Norate...

Selma closed her eyes for a moment, and a hologram of

Selma watching the Jacobson Movement documentary that is aired every New Year's Day appeared above her head, the narrator's voice bellowing in surround sound: *All Jacobson representatives are referred to by their order of employment in each department, rather than their real name. An acronym plus a number. For example, all employees of the Neural Oscillation Registry will have a prefix of NOR. The number refers to their hierarchy status.*

Nor8, then...*Nor8, Nor8, Nor8...*

The hologram disappeared and the narrator's voice was replaced with Selma's: *What association does someone at PremsBank have with the Neural Oscillation Registry? Is she manipulating our emotions?*

"Yes, I am," Norate said, without interrupting her stride or turning around. "But not intrusively. I will not manipulate your thoughts, simply the way you feel about them."

Selma looked up and behind. "Can everyone hear my thoughts in here?" Selma whispered.

"No. Just you and me. It's the same for Leila. I can also communicate with the both of you at the same time without interference. If you like, we can have a conversation about that after the impregnation as everyone who works for Governor Jacobson has taken an oath to be completely transparent. There are no secrets here, Mrs. Beyett."

Selma fell silent.

Norate laughed in consolation. "I can also feel your feelings."

Selma blushed, noticed Leila's calm smile, and gently took her hand.

"My role in the initiation of this process is to ensure you both remain stress free," Norate said. "The successful fertilization of Leila's egg relies heavily on her having a positive outlook and feeling relaxed. There is nothing at all to worry about Mrs. Beyett. And to add to your silent observation, it *was* like this thirteen years ago, but it was all hidden."

"Why?"

"Governor Jacobson was afraid of a revolt if people found things out for themselves before they were ready. But he insisted that hiding the truth would benefit no-one. He was right. Some may not like the way the Globe is run, but they will always believe what is said."

Norate stopped walking and turned to face them.

"We are here." Norate bent down and cupped Leila's cheeks in her hands, looking her directly in the eyes. "Today is a magical day," she said. "Today is your first step toward the Second Life Phase, where you will live in eternal harmony."

"Thank you. Thank you so much," Leila said in a tone seldom associated with any teenage girl. It was a tone of complete awareness and selflessness—of herself, of those around her, and of the Globe. Norate and Leila nodded in unison before Norate continued down the tunnel on her own. Selma blinked and suddenly she was standing by Leila, who was lying on a bed. It was Leila's bed in Leila's room. They had replicated her bedroom. Everything was exactly the same, except for its tidiness and the medical equipment lined along the back wall.

A woman entered through a real door. "Hello Leila. Hello Mrs. Beyett." She was wearing a large shiny silver pendant with a capital D on it. "I'm Dr. Premsten and I'm going to give you a life today, Leila. How are you feeling?"

Leila smiled. "I feel great."

"That's wonderful, Leila. Mrs. Beyett, would you like to remain by Leila's side for the procedure?"

Selma nodded. "Please."

"Okey dokey. That's perfectly fine, but I'm going to have to ask that you take a seat over there as I'm afraid you aren't allowed to touch her."

Selma frowned.

"We can't allow your energy to come in contact with Leila's. It will interfere with her hormone balance, which can lead to miscarriage."

Selma took a deep breath and nodded her understanding. She went to sit on the armchair in the far corner of the room, which was usually filled with abandoned teddy bears at home. As she rubbed her knees and closed her eyes, the sound of trickling water surrounded her. When she opened her eyes, she saw that a glass casement was generating at high speed around her. She tried to jump out of her seat with a muted gasp, but a magnetic force held her down.

"What's going on?" Selma started to shout, but then lowered her voice at the sight of Leila, still and helpless on the bed.

"Please," Dr. Premsten said, her lips not moving. "Your daughter is in good hands, and no harm will come to her. Just sit and relax. This is all just protocol. We have had too many mothers tragically interfere with the procedure. It is for Leila's own good. And yours. Please trust me."

Dr. Premsten lifted Leila's shirt and rubbed clear jelly all over her stomach. Saliva built up around the walls of Selma's mouth as she clenched her teeth. "Mrs. Beyett, would you like me to call Norate to help you relax?"

Selma swallowed and shook her head, muttering, "Relax, relax, relax" under her breath.

"Hundreds of impregnations happen every day without a fault, Selma," Dr. Premsten continued. "And the Jacobson Movement is one hundred percent transparent, just as Norate informed you earlier. If you need anything at any time, all you have to do is think."

Dr. Premsten dimmed the lights, picked up a syringe filled with a clear liquid and placed it inside a metal tray on the bedside table. She pulled the ultrasound monitor toward her then slowly moved her hovering hand over Leila's abdomen. Images of Leila's uterus and ovaries transmitted to the screen in crystal clear resolution. With her hand still hovering above Leila's abdomen, Dr. Premsten pressed the corner of the screen. The image zoomed in and in until the inside of an ovary was visible. An egg appeared and escaped from the ovary into the uterus. Dr. Premsten wiped her hand with a light blue woolen towel. The image locked on the screen despite Dr. Premsten removing her hand.

"Leila, I am now going to give you an injection into your belly. It may sting a very little bit, but it will be over as quick as it starts, okay?"

Leila nodded with the same serene smile spread across her face. Dr. Premsten inserted the needle. Leila didn't flinch.

"Warnings are just protocol, Selma," Dr. Premsten said, her lips not parting at all.

Selma sighed with relief.

"Leila, I'm going to leave the room for a few minutes now and give your body some time to do its job. Just close your eyes and count to one hundred. Can you do that for me?

"Yep," Leila mouthed.

"Okey dokey. It won't be long now. Try and stay—calm." Dr. Premsten left the room, smiling on her way past at Selma's expression of concern.

Just as the doctor closed the door behind her, Leila wriggled and moaned like she had done in the past when down with a fever.

Selma's heartbeat echoed around the room in unison with Leila's.

Leila's breath quickened as she groaned in pain. She attempted to sit up, but couldn't. She thrashed around and grabbed at the sheet covering her, scrunched it in her fists and cried, "Mum, it hurts! Make it stop!"

"Leila? What's happening? What are you feeling?" Selma was finally able to break free from the armchair, but couldn't get through the glass wall that surrounded her. She thumped the glass and it echoed through the room like a jackhammer under water. "What's going on? What have you done to her?" Selma screamed, her words catching in her throat. "Let me out! Let me go to her!"

"Mrs. Beyett, Leila is not being harmed in any way." Norate appeared in front of Selma and she flattened her hands against the glass. "Touch your hands to my hands."

Leila's wails grew louder and louder, her body and limbs still thrashing about. She tried to get up again, but couldn't move a single part of her body more than a couple of inches away from the mattress. It looked like she was having a seizure.

Selma begged, "What's happening to her? Please tell me what's happening to her?"

"Hold your hands to my hands and look me in the eye, Selma," Norate said robotically, with a strange air of controlled empathy.

"Why should I do that? You're just going to calm me down and it won't be real."

"I will do no such thing. I'm going to make you understand. That is all."

Selma's tears streamed down her face as she shook her head.

"Please," Norate said. "I know this is hard for you to see. It won't last long. I promise. Touch your hands to my hands, Selma. Touch your hands to my hands. Please."

Selma glanced at Leila, who had stopped moving but still moaned in pain, and did as Norate asked.

"Leila's fertilization and first trimester are being accelorated to avoid miscarriage. It hurts because the child is growing very quickly inside her. There will be no complications. Her body is built to deal with the rapid transformation. The pain will subside once the acceleration stops at the level of a four-month fetus." Norate turned to look at the monitor and Leila had stopped moaning. "Which is now."

Norate removed her hands and the glass trickled away. Selma ran to Leila, held her in her arms, and kissed her head. "Sweetheart, I'm so sorry. I'm so sorry I put you through that. We should have waited like you said. I should have listened to you. I'm so—" Leila pushed Selma away and turned her back to her.

Norate rested a hand on Selma's shoulder, but Selma removed it like it was a dirty cloth.

"You said you were transparent here, Norate. You said there were no secrets."

"That's right. We have no secrets."

"Then what do you call this?" Selma said gritting her teeth.

"Mrs. Beyett, I am quite certain that I relayed all necessary information to you. If I neglected to tell you something, please do bring the issue to my attention and I shall have no qualms in disclosing the requested information in full."

"*Now* you've told me! What about before? Why didn't you tell me what was going to happen in here *before* it happened?"

"Mrs. Beyett, I'm afraid you did not ask. It is not my duty to grant you the knowledge of the Globe if it is not requested. I did everything I was required to do to keep you calm."

Selma glared at Norate.

"Truth is indisputable and unchangeable," Norate added. "There is no point in arguing with logic. Besides, what good would it do? It's over. It's done."

"Over? Done? Leila is going to be eternally traumatized!"

"Mrs. Beyett, I'm terribly sorry that this day has ended in distress for you. I would offer to assist in calming you, but I'm afraid I'm forbidden to engage in recreational relaxation. Can I perhaps offer you a free tour of our meditation lab?"

"Why was I anesthetized?"

Norate stared blankly at Selma for a moment. "I'm sorry. I don't quite follow."

"When I was impregnated with Leila. Why was I anesthetized and why wasn't my pregnancy accelerated in this way?"

"Because, Mrs. Beyett, too many women were miscarrying. Science has come a long way in thirteen years."

Selma looked at the ceiling and blinked back tears. "I have more questions. But right now I just want to take Leila home. To her *real* bedroom. I will be lodging an official complaint."

"I'm sorry to hear that," Norate said. "But before I leave you I need to ask whether Leila intends to marry a donor. She has the privilege of being able to choose the biological father today, as he is single. Or if she prefers, we can give her a list of other suitable candidates."

"I don't think she knows what she wants yet," Selma snapped, sniffing and wiping her nose. "When does she have to decide?"

"She has until the birth of her child to make a decision. A form will be sent to her to fill in and lodge at the Tall. If she chooses to remain single, she will have to sign a document which officially cancels her lifetime healthcare benefits. If she chooses to marry, the donor or other candidate will be notified immediately, and a ceremony date will be set by a Tall official. Information on how to proceed further will be forwarded once the documents are signed."

"Right," Selma nodded curtly. "Can we go now?"

"Please stay until Leila wakes up naturally. From this point on it is safe for Leila to resume life as normal. Please be sure to collect Leila's Fertilization Certificate on the way out along with the official statement relating to the healthcare monetary supplement you have been granted. Dr. Premsten will be waiting for you at the entrance with the documents. And ... congratulations."

Selma squinted. "Not sure becoming a grandmother is worthy of congratulations nowadays, is it?" She crossed her arms and sat at the foot of the bed. Leila was still fast asleep.

"Oh, not for that, Mrs. Beyett. Congratulations on finding happiness."

LISTEN

You must really want to know what happens next with Selma, Jerome and Leila. The look on your face is priceless, Eve. I suppose you also need more time to warm to me. It's fine, I don't blame you. I was a pretty cold person too, back then. I hated the Jacobson Movement because I felt trapped, socially abused and discriminated against for taking control of my own life. And I must admit that I also probably liked to go against the grain just for the sake of it, mainly because a lot of people those days had way too much trust and faith in the government that they'd stopped asking questions and lived like robots, accepting their fates. I couldn't stop asking questions. My parents taught me well. So please, Eve, don't give up yet. Just keep listening and it will all start making sense soon.

That morning at the bakery when Selma asked me her big question, it changed me. It changed the way I looked at the Globe and our purpose on it. It changed the way I looked at the Jacobson Movement. It may not seem big when you hear it right now, but it will in a minute. Patience is a virtue. Isn't that what they used to say?

"Will you help Jerome?" Selma asked.

"How do you mean?" I said, with my mouth half-full of cake.

Selma stood up and walked to the counter. She pulled an

envelope out of her bag, sat back down and handed it to me. I took it. Opened it. Read it.

I looked up at her. Selma didn't look happy. She looked miserable.

"Does this make sense to you?" I asked.

Selma shook her head and started to cry again. "No. It doesn't. It doesn't make sense at all. I don't even have a career. They said I would need a fulfilling and successful career to reach this point in the FLP. I honestly hadn't expected to make it."

"You think it's the bakery?" I said. How could it have been anything else?

"I don't know. I really don't know. I'm so confused. This..." she gestured around the bakery. "This was never a dream of mine. I just opened it because I got bored of being a stay-at-home mother and enjoyed baking cakes for Leila."

"So you enjoy it?"

Selma nodded. "Yes, but—"

"Then it must simply be because you enjoy your work."

"But I enjoyed doing it at home before this."

"But at home it's not a job."

Selma looked toward the front door. My morning's work walked in and she quickly wiped away her tears and put on a smile. While Selma served the customer, I wondered how she thought I would be able help her husband. But her position also made me think. If she could find happiness without a lifetime spent preparing for it, then maybe I still had a chance. Maybe I didn't have to do this tit-for-tat shit forever, and perhaps I should just give working a go? As long as I kept my expectations low, as long as it was only about providing better care for my son, then if I got a letter like Selma's it would just be a welcome bonus.

Selma waved the customer off with her purchases and the

door chimed as she sat back down and rubbed her floury hands on her knees. She picked up the conversation as if there hadn't been any pause.

"Maybe you're right. I hope you're right, because that means Jerome has a chance too. Icasia, I can't go to my Transition Grave without him there, I just can't. When I thought I didn't have a chance of making it, I never considered the idea. I thought I would just be annihilated at 60.0. I had accepted it. That's a good enough life. But now? Now the death inducement age is so young, and I could end up going through it without having Jerome on the other side. I can't live in limbo alone. I wouldn't be able to cope."

Selma burst into tears and ran into the kitchen. I could hear her tearing off kitchen towel and muffling her sobs with it. I followed her in there. She was sitting on the floor in a mess of dough scraps and moistened icing sugar. For a second, I could only think about how dirty her butt would be when she got up.

I sat down beside her and stroked her hair. Seeing her break down like this made me feel a little closer to her. I loved Abel more than anything on the Globe, and I couldn't imagine anyone even suggesting that he might be taken away.

I will never forget the first time I read him *Ten Little Fingers and Ten Little Toes*. He was just sixteen months old. I sat him on my lap, pointing to the pictures of all the different babies on each page, my stomach sinking in the knowledge that he would never have a little brother or sister to play with, like the kid in this picture book.

With each new page, each new picture and each new sentence, Abel would reply, "Hmm." He'd point to what I was pointing to and look up at me for confirmation. When I reached the climax of the story, and uttered the words, *the*

*next baby born was truly divine, a sweet little child, who was
mine, all mine. And this little baby, as everyone knows, has
ten little fingers, ten little toes, and three little kisses on the
tip of his nose.*

And instead of me kissing Abel's nose, he turned around
and kissed mine.

I was still a child myself then, but I will never ever forget
how it made my young heart melt. He was mine. All mine.
And there was no way I was ever going to let him go.

I thought about this moment, and immediately knew I had
to help them.

"Tell me how to help and I'll do my best," I said.

"Can you help us find the way to Jerome's happiness?"

I laughed. I couldn't help it. It was like she was asking me
to tell him the meaning of life.

"I can't do it on my own," she said after seeing the baffled
look on my face. "I'm too close to him. I can't see things
objectively."

"Are you sure you're asking the right person? I mean, look
at me. I'm a tatter. I don't play by the rules, I dress like
a gypsy, I have no concept of what it takes to succeed in
a career, I have no goals or ambitions. My heart is pretty
much dry. So why me?"

"Your heart is not dry."

I smiled and glanced out the window into a private yard
full of overflowing rubbish bags. "You think I'm here because
I like you? I'm here because you feed my son."

Selma sniffed, wiped her eyes, and did something
completely unexpected. She hugged me. It was warm and
genuine and soothing. It was a hug like my mother used to
give me when I came home to my son empty-handed. The
hug said it didn't matter, that it was the effort that counted,
that Abel wouldn't starve if he had to wait one more day,
and he wouldn't love me any less.

I didn't quite know how to react to the hug, and it took me a few moments with my arms sticking out to my sides before I reciprocated. Even then, when I did wrap my arms around Selma, I couldn't bring myself to hold her as tightly and firmly as she was holding me.

"You are exactly the person we need," Selma said. "You live your life in constant survival mode. You generate smarter ideas a lot faster than people who live by the Book and who are given everything they need on a silver platter. So yes, it's you I need. I don't need you to care. I need your survival skills." Selma stood and hovered above me now. "But I think you do care. You just can't admit it to yourself."

I felt small and insignificant. She'd made me shed a layer of protective skin. I didn't know whether to admit that she was right out loud. I had to get up off the floor and prove somehow that I hadn't gone soft.

She held out her hand. I grabbed it and she pulled me to my feet. Neither of us wiped off our clothes. I stood next to her, staring out the window again, at the overflowing garbage bags, too nervous to look her in the eye just yet. I am like those bags, I thought. I'll be full of all sorts of garbage until I get taken to the tip if I keep living like this. Maybe this is a chance for something more. Maybe by helping Jerome I can help myself.

I looked at Selma, ready to tell her that I would do it, but I didn't have to say anything. She could see it in my face.

Selma took a deep breath with both hands covering her face. I could tell she was smiling as well because her cheeks were puffed up. She removed her hands from her face, winked, turned me around, wiped my pants down with a damp cloth and said, "Are you hungry? I baked the most delicious quiche this morning."

The quiche was made with goat's cheese and watercress

and literally melted in my mouth. I devoured it within minutes. When I finished and wiped my mouth with the hem of my t-shirt, ignoring the napkin next to my plate, Selma hadn't even got through half of hers.

Selma chuckled and said, "Why do you eat so fast? I swear I get indigestion just watching you."

"Habit, I guess." I shrugged. "Always on the go." Then I burped. My face flushed and Selma chuckled again.

"I think this calls for some wine. Red or white?"

I glanced at the inTel to see the time. "At eleven in the morning?"

"Time is relative where alcohol is concerned."

"I really shouldn't. I have to get moving onto my next tat."

Selma feigned a frown with a simultaneous half-smile and clicked her fingers as if she'd just had an idea. I knew it was totally put on, but not in a sly way. Sure, she had plans for me, but she was the first person I had ever met that seemed to genuinely want to help me.

"What would you say if I said you didn't ever have to tit-for-tat for food again?"

"I'd say I wouldn't be able to accept that offer." There was no way I wanted to be in debt. Not to anyone. Even if I liked them and trusted them—even if they didn't want me to pay them back.

"Why not?"

I hesitated. I told her the closest I could bring myself to the truth. "Because ... I mean ... I really don't think what I can offer you deserves such kindness." Well, okay, you're right, Eve, that was also true.

"Don't think of it as an exchange. It's not. Think of it as a completely selfish act. I want you to stay here with me during opening hours, so clearly, I need to feed your family to get that. I'm ... pretty much purchasing your company." Selma's mouth went wonky and she laughed nervously.

"I have never realized," she said, "how pathetic I must seem until this moment." She spun to the left, about to get out of her seat, but paused, spread her fingers in front of her and stared at them for a while.

"Okay," I whispered, noticing the absence of her wedding ring. "Red."

Selma didn't look at me. She smiled at her hands, flexed her fingers a few times and headed to the kitchen. She returned with a bottle of red wine without a label and a couple of beautiful crystal glasses that looked like the ones in the movies from the olden days that the Mafia drank scotch from.

"Sorry, I don't have wine glasses," Selma said. "But these were here when I bought the place, and I think they're lovely." Selma poured the wine and we toasted our business deal. I think Selma was strategically humoring me. I wasn't quite ready to be proper friends yet, and I'm sure she knew it.

We sipped on our wine and didn't talk for about fifteen minutes. My silence must have been disconcerting for her. It definitely was for me. I didn't know whether I was doing the right thing. One, I didn't like being dependent on people. Two, I didn't like others being dependent on me in such a big way—especially when I had no idea if I was going to be able to deliver. Three, I didn't have friends. Now, I don't mean that I didn't have friends because people didn't like me, I mean that I didn't have friends by choice. Selfishness has no place in a friendship. And I, at the time, had no concept of altruism, even in its smallest form. Even after everything I had heard from Selma, even after discovering I was needed to save a marriage and a *life*, I was still in it for myself and my son. I wanted to use the experience to better *our* life, not Selma's. But it's early in my story. If you're starting to hate me, Eve, I crave your patience.

"I think we need to do this gradually," Selma said, after swallowing the last drop of wine from her glass.

"Uh ..."

"Jerome can't know that you are actually helping. He'll clam up. He hates other people knowing his business."

I shrugged. "Sure. What do you have in mind?"

"Well, tonight we're all going to my parents' Grave Vanishing Ceremony. I think you should come. I'll introduce you to Jerome and Leila and tell them I've taken you on as a baking assistant and customer services manager."

"But I'm not. Won't that cause problems with your books?"

"Not at all. He doesn't interfere with my work and I don't interfere with his. It's the most risk-free solution. If I say you're my friend, he'll be suspicious. I've never introduced him to anyone. Ever. He'll be suspicious as it is, but it's close to the truth, at least."

I started to feel we had more in common than I'd originally thought.

"Okay, sure. But what's your reason for bringing an assistant along to celebrate your parents' transition?" I asked. "It's a bit personal, isn't it?"

Selma smiled. Clearly, she had already predicted potential obstacles and figured out all the answers. "You're also an aspiring writer doing research for a work in progress. I invited you because I thought it would help you get one step closer to the Second Life Phase. Jerome would appreciate that. And I think—"

"Wait a minute. An aspiring writer?"

"Yes. You look like one."

"Do I?"

"Yes." Selma was laughing now.

I wasn't sure whether to take it as a compliment or a criticism. Most writers were strange pompous know-it-alls underneath their lazy gypsy-like attire. But everyone on the Globe admired them. They were highly regarded and often invited to present their findings at Jacobian events. They're quite rare nowadays, too, given that most entertainment literature is computer generated. Any real writers that exist are only permitted to write nonfiction that will benefit the Globe. I guess they're more like what people would have called journalists in the olden days.

"What if he asks me questions about my book?"

"That's easy. You just tell him it's very much a first draft at the moment and you don't feel comfortable sharing. He'll respect that."

I nodded, with a wonky grin on my face. Suddenly I felt like this was a legitimate truth about me. I *felt* like a writer. It would be fun pretending to be one.

"It will also give you an opportunity to ask Jerome questions. I can sort of take you under my wing a bit. Invite you around for dinner. Give you a reason to be in his life."

I laughed and muffled the sound with a fist. I couldn't believe I was going to do this. It was exciting. I could scarcely grasp the consequences of what I was diving into. It just felt like an exciting game. My life didn't often lend itself to exploring something that might be fun, so it was a luxury.

"Okay. It sounds cool. But I should at least have a book title so that the questions I ask him sound relevant, right?"

"Yes! Great point. See? Survival skills. You're already using them."

The compliment made me blush and I downed the rest of my wine to try and hide it.

"Right, let's see." Selma squeezed her nose and held her breath as though it helped her to think. "It has to be something that doesn't directly ask him about his career," she said, still holding her nose closed so she sounded like a duck.

Then she released it and sniffed. "He's too switched on ... what do you think—"

"How about," I said, wavering, interrupting, wanting to prove myself before I even had a solid idea. The words that followed were a complete spur-of-the-moment fluke. "How about, *The Pros and Cons of Living Beyond the Book.*"

"Oh, my goodness!" Selma bolted upright and clapped her hands together. "That's genius!"

I blushed again. "I'm not sure about genius, but it's a start."

"It *is* genius. That is absolutely something Governor Jacobson would want to publish to try and convince more people to become Dependents. And the fact that you don't live by the Book yourself is excellent, because it can be a bit like a collection of case studies inspired by your own life. Yes! That's ideal."

"It also sounds like a book I'd be interested in reading," I said with a chuckle, pouring myself some more wine. The way Selma talked to me, and the way I was behaving in her company made me feel like a real citizen. I had been given a taste of middle class living, and I wanted more.

Selma wrote down the details of the Grave Vanishing Ceremony that night for me and I promised not to be late. In fact, I was early, and I managed to eavesdrop on Jerome and his father having a one-to-one chat in front of his mother's Transition Grave.

I'd never been to the Anima Cemetery before and was stunned by the giant statues of Thanatos and Hypnos rising up on either side of the entrance.

You probably haven't learned about Thanatos and Hypnos, Eve, so let me explain how symbolic those statues were.

According to Greek Mythology, Thanatos and Hypnos were twin brothers and were born of Chaos, the churning mass of energy that gave birth to the universe. They had power over the physical world and the hidden world—such as Day, Night, Sky and our Globe. To the Greeks they were handsome winged gods, bringers of peace and serenity. Hypnos controlled the land of dreams and Thanatos guided the dead to the afterlife. Thanatos and Hypnos had agreed that when gods walked upon the Globe, they would not interfere in the lives of mortals. However, as much as they tried to honor their vows, when selfish leaders tried to tilt the balance of power to plot against mankind, they found they could not stand by and do nothing,

Greek mythology aside, I thought these statues quite symbolic in other ways too. The fact that they were brothers was yet another push for family union by Governor Jacobson, and simultaneously a slap in the face—a reminder that we brought the current state of the world upon ourselves, because these days siblings very rarely know of each's existence.

I stepped inside Anima Cemetery and lost my balance a little. I thought I was hallucinating for a second, but then realized that the floor, walls and ceiling were completely covered with a projection of the sky. I was walking on clouds. Something I thought I'd only ever experience in my dreams.

It took a minute to summon up enough courage to move. Before I stepped forward, a bluebird hovered in front of me, chirped, and somehow I ended up following it across the lobby toward a never-ending warehouse of glass urns. For a moment I thought the actual glass was blue, but then I saw swirls of blue moving inside them like miniature gusts of wind.

My heart skipped a beat.

They were *souls*. People's souls, just like mine and yours, waiting for their offspring to follow in their footsteps so they could be released into the Second Life Phase. Do they feel time? I wondered. Space? Longing? Were they burdened by waiting? Could they see, smell, taste and touch? Could they hear us talking about them when we visited? Were they suppressed ghosts? Was this Hades or Purgatory?

This place of peace and serenity suddenly felt like ... iced fire.

"Son, you need this for yourself first and foremost."

A man's voice came out of nowhere. I looked around, even *up*, but all I saw was cloud and sky.

"I don't want it," another man said.

"Sure, you do, son. Somewhere, deep inside you, is a reason to live. You'll find it."

"You sure about that, Dad?" he laughed.

It occurred to me that it might be Jerome, and I spotted a small silhouette in the distance, reaching to take something from a wall of urns. I squinted, and vaguely made him out as he removed one from the wall.

Their voices were rather loud, despite being so far away, and I wondered how it was possible.

"Because everything is possible in limbo," a woman whispered in my ear from behind. I gasped in shock and spun around.

"Who are you?"

"My name is Acsix. I am the designated host for the ceremony of Selma's parents. You are here for her."

The assertion was disconcerting. As if I was being brainwashed. I knew I wasn't. I *was* there for Selma, but shouldn't it have been a question? And what was Selma doing telling this woman why I was here?

"Oh," Acsix giggled. "She did no such thing. Your thoughts are shifting, that is all."

"Pardon?"

"Your thoughts are shifting."

I nodded, pretending to understand, too afraid to ask. I came for a transition ceremony, and I had walked into a world I had no idea existed. I mean, I knew there was something bigger, grander, more extravagant, but no idea what. I needed time to catch my breath.

"Would you like me to take you to Mr. Beyett and his father?" Acsix asked.

I shook my head. Muted. I hadn't even been introduced to them. It would have been awkward.

"Would you like to be taken to a waiting room? I'll tell Selma you are in there."

I shook my head again, like a mischievous child.

Acsix giggled again. "Suit yourself. I'll make sure Selma finds you."

I nodded. Acsix grinned and bit her top lip.

"Uh ..." I wavered. "Can Jerome hear my thoughts too?" The whole plan Selma and I had concocted was not going to work if he could.

Acsix laughed. "No. For the time being only Jacobson staff can thought-shift with visitors. We can also receive thought data from civilians if they are within a 50-meter radius of a Jacobson organization."

I lifted my eyebrows in question.

"It enables us to get ahead of potential intruders."

I sighed in relief and wondered what kind of intruders she was talking about.

"It also prevents government corruption when we can receive each other's thought data. I'm sure you have heard that Governor Jacobson thrives on honesty."

I squinted at Acsix, not too convinced about the honesty

thing. What government could possibly be 100 percent honorable?

"Yes. Well." Acsix cleared her throat. "Receiving civilian thought data prevents crime. It also enables us to answer your questions quickly and effectively, and to make clear judgements." Acsix squinted back at me as if I'd offended her and walked away without warning.

"Look, son," Jerome's father said. "Of course, I want to see your mother again. But most of all I want your mother to have the chance to transition. She's been cooped up in here for Jacob knows how long. The only luck she ever had on this Globe was giving birth to you, and both of us receiving the Letter. She's come this far. *We've* come this far. Could you really bear it if you denied us a chance of SLP?"

Jerome scoffed. "Thanks, Dad. Thanks so much for keeping the pressure off."

"I'm sorry, son. I'm sorry. But that's just the way it is."

Silence hung in the air for a few moments before Jerome sniffed as if he were crying.

"Dad, don't you care about me at all? You haven't once mentioned my wellbeing, you know that?"

"I'm sorry, son. It wasn't intentional. You've lost faith in yourself. I thought a bit of perspective might help."

"Perspective?" Jerome groaned. "Well, Dad, thanks for the perspective. You've made my survival seem very important to you."

"Son—"

"No, Dad. Just stop." Jerome handed the urn to his father. "Here. Maybe it's best you say goodbye. Another opportunity to visit might never be on the cards."

Jerome walked away and disappeared into the distance.

I had no idea Jerome was so set on totally giving up. One thing was for sure, though, that dude was not going to be persuaded to survive by inflicting guilt. Brilliant, I thought. Just brilliant. Inflicting guilt—making people feel it's their *duty* to help—was my specialty. I honestly thought I'd be able to use that skill, but I realized I was going to have to get a lot more creative.

Right, I thought. I nodded and straightened my jacket sleeves. I said to myself: *Make him like you. Be friendly and appreciative. Don't prod. Let him be the first to open up so that whatever you say is a response to him. That's respectful. That's decent. That's the way to do it.*

You might think I was being manipulative, Eve, but you'll see, in the end, it was the only way.

WATCH

"Acsix. Excuse me," Selma snapped, clutching her parents' empty urns close to her chest. "How many complaints do I have to make about you people? Why wasn't I informed that my parents would already have transitioned before the ceremony?"

"Mrs. Beyett, I must apologize that you weren't aware of this. But this information is common knowledge."

"Common knowledge? And how do you suppose it can be considered common knowledge when every human being only has one chance to experience this?"

Acsix blushed. Selma placed the urns on the low coffee table by her knees. She crossed her arms and stood between Jerome and Leila, who were on a sofa facing in opposite directions.

"It's written in the Jacobson Guide, and it's also been broadcast on the inTel. We are unable to control the speed at which a soul wishes to travel once permission for its release is transmitted, Mrs. Beyett. You cannot hold me to blame for your lack of interest in current affairs." Selma's mouth opened, but only a small croak escaped. Acsix turned swiftly on her heel and said, half facing away, "I shall return momentarily. I suggest you all take a moment to think about the true meaning of the ceremony today. Life is not dependent on palpability. It is dependent on awareness."

Acsix left the room. Jerome stood and held Selma in his arms.

"I should write another letter of complaint. She was rude, wasn't she? Plain rude!"

Jerome tried to console Selma, "At least they're there. You should be grateful."

Selma struggled out of Jerome's embrace and poked him in the chest. "How dare you. This is *my* moment. The only one I'll ever experience. How *dare* you insinuate that it's less important than your situation."

Leila sighed and mumbled under her breath, "He's always been selfish."

Selma groaned. "Leila, he has not. You apologize to your father."

"It's okay. I deserved it," Jerome said, pinching the bridge of his nose. "She's right. All the more reason to give up."

"Jerome, stop it. Leila, apologize. Now."

Leila scrunched up her mouth, shook her head, looked at her slightly swollen stomach and rubbed circles around her belly button. The quiet motion triggered a smile. One of those smiles that live in another time and space.

"I can't wait to get away from them," Leila whispered to her stomach. "No more fights. No more rules. You're a baby girl, aren't you? I just know it. I will never ever marry. It will just be me and you, baby girl. Just me and you."

"Jome ..." Selma softened her voice and placed her hands on Jerome's chest. "How do you expect to gain her love and respect if you keep agreeing with her insults?"

"She'll never love me, Sma. I think the last five years have established that. Anyway, *I'm* sorry. I shouldn't have switched the focus onto me today."

Selma smiled in forgiveness.

"I talked to Dad," Jerome said. "He tried to help me, but he made me feel worse."

"I'm sure he didn't mean it."

Jerome smiled. "I know. But I'm beginning to realize where I may have inherited this relentless selfishness from."

Selma scoffs. "Where is Gary anyway?"

Jerome switched the weight between his feet. "I told him to leave."

"Oh, Jome ..." Selma squeezed Jerome's shoulder and glanced at Leila, who was still smiling and stroking her stomach. "I think we should go home, too."

Jerome frowned. "What about the ceremony?"

"As much as I think that Acsix is a disrespectful little rodent, she was probably right about one thing."

Jerome puckered his brow in question.

"Life is about awareness, not palpability. In which case, who needs a ceremony when I have their memory?"

Jerome ran his thumb along Selma's right brow and kissed her on the lips. His lips had hardly touched hers when she yanked herself away.

"Dammit."

"What's wrong?"

"I forgot that my, uh, assistant from the bakery is meeting us here."

"You have an assistant?"

"I know, I know, I should have told you about her—"

"Just invite her over for dinner."

LISTEN

"That would be lovely," I said, entering the waiting room with my head held high and my hand outstretched for Jerome to shake. Shyness had no place in this situation. I had to be the professional. I had to be a strong-minded and cultured writer.

Selma looked shocked by my entrance, but it didn't take her long to play along.

"Jerome, meet Icasia."

"Pleased to meet you, Jerome," I said, taking his warm sweaty hand in mine.

"The pleasure is all mine," Jerome said, shaking my hand with a huge smile on his face. He seemed sweet, kind ... tortured, his handshake at the same time strong and welcoming yet loose and indifferent. When he released his grip, I resisted the urge to wipe my hand on my jeans.

"And this," Selma said gesturing to her daughter who seemed totally lost in space, "is Leila."

I stared. Too long, I think. At the expression of calm that masked an inner unease. She was in a trance, her eyes focused on something and nothing. My stomach sank at the near replica of myself when I was pregnant with Abel. It was as if I'd travelled back in time, looking at my own reflection. The fear, the sense of constraint and unfamiliarity shone so fiercely in her eyes that it resembled the moving souls in the glass urns. But joy shone just as brightly through her smile. This exact juxtaposition of emotions grounded me during pregnancy, and that marked the point where I decided I would not conform.

"Icasia?" Selma touched my elbow and I blinked free from my cocoon of speculation.

"I'm sorry," I shook my head and cooled my flushed cheeks with my hands. "Leila, it's lovely to meet you too. Your dress is rather beautiful. I had one just like it when I was your age."

Leila looked me directly in the eyes, blinked, and smiled. It was a different smile now. More a signal of thanks than anything else. But I was sure it was genuine.

"Leila, you don't mind if I join you for dinner, do you?" I thought it better to ask her myself, to show I respected her feelings. It would also show Jerome that I respected his family and make it easier for him to accept me into his home.

"You're pretty," Leila said.

I think I blushed. "Thank you. So are you."

Leila definitely blushed.

"I like her," Leila said to Selma, raising her eyebrows in affirmation.

Jerome stepped back slightly as if he had no place in this conversation. But something inside me made me think he was laughing inside and trying to hide it. I had no reason to dislike Jerome, but he seemed like the odd one out, and there was a fire in his eyes that I couldn't quite place. Looking back now, I believe it was simply a case of harmless envy, but I remember thinking then that he had an agenda, which made me curious—and somewhat protective of Leila, whom I'd warmed to immediately.

Selma glanced at Jerome and then at me, took a deep

breath and clapped her hands together. "Right. I've got some fabulous plans for dinner. Let me notify Acsix that her services are no longer needed and then we can head off."

"Just think in her general direction," I said. "She'll get the picture."

Leila laughed out loud, and stood up and walked toward me. She took my hand, looked up at me and grinned. She said, "I'm glad you're joining us. Maybe you can help Mum and me look for an apartment online after we eat?"

"Sure, I'd love that," I said. But I regretted it immediately when I realized Leila was trying to provoke Jerome.

He quickly hung his head and turned, hiding this emotional stab wound.

But he wasn't quick enough to hide the tear that rolled down his cheek.

Leila sat next to me during dinner. Occasionally she would sway toward me and rest the top of her head on my upper arm every time she'd laugh at a joke I hadn't known I'd told. I'd snatch glances at Jerome when this happened. He usually smiled into his plate and stuffed his mouth with too much food. Selma kept winking at me when Jerome wasn't looking. I wanted to tell her to stop. That she was being too obvious. That I could handle this. But maybe it was just obvious to me.

The apricot-colored tablecloth was crisp and freshly washed, and it didn't hang off the edges of the table properly. I kept catching my knuckles on it every time I brought my right hand above the table, almost spilling my mango juice every time. Of course, this made Leila laugh while Jerome continued to fake his smiles.

"Not every single thing Icasia says is funny, Leila. Stop overreacting, will you?" His tone wasn't stern. He said it in a cute teasing way with a smirk on his face.

"Fuck off, Dad."

Selma gasped, clapped a hand to her mouth, and Jerome craned his neck inwards. He squinted at Leila as if he was peering at her from over a pair of spectacles.

Selma looked to Jerome for guidance, and her mouth opened and shut a few times. Jerome cleared his throat and Leila looked down into her lap with a victorious smirk. It only took a moment though, for the smirk to disappear and be replaced with the energy of regret and disappointment in herself.

Very few people said *fuck* anymore. To me it belonged in the cartoon dialogue of the Jacobson Daily Herald. I had no idea where Leila might have heard it, or even discovered the context in which to use it. But I have to tell you, it impressed me. I wanted to launch into a conversation about linguistics.

I leaned to my left and spoke as softly as possible. "Don't sweat it." I shrugged and scrunched up my nose. "It's the pregnancy. Maybe let her be excused? She's probably tired."

Selma swallowed and glanced at Jerome. He nodded.

"Leila, you may go to your room." Jerome really didn't have a clue about how to phrase things in a way that didn't provoke a hormonal teenager to retaliate.

"Why should I go to my room? It's just a word," Leila spat. "And besides, since when is speaking your mind against the rules in this house?"

"Honey, your father didn't mean it like that. He is just letting you—"

Leila stood up so fast that her chair tipped backwards and it hit the floor with a smack. "He's *not* my *fucking* father!" she screamed and stared directly at Jerome. Why didn't Jerome stick up for himself? He was the parent, even if not biologically, but that wasn't exactly unique in this day and age. He should have asserted more authority, at least in my opinion. There was no way I would let my son talk to *any*one like that, regardless of the relationship.

Selma and Jerome seemed tongue-tied. I wondered whether it was because I was there, or whether Leila's behavior was inconsistent with her usual self. Nonetheless, I felt it was time to intervene.

"Leila, why don't you show me your room and I can show you a few pictures of my son." I squeezed Selma's hand under the table, and she squeezed mine back and mouthed, *thank you.*

Leila sat on the edge of her bed, her small belly stretching the waist of her nightdress a little, and let out a sigh of relief. I'd always wondered what it would be like to have a daughter, but seeing all the heartache Selma was going through dealing with PremsBank made me glad I'd had a boy.

"He's not my real father, you know," Leila said. "He's a—"

"Monster?" I replied.

"Yes!" Leila's eyes lit up and she bounced a little on the mattress.

I sat next to her. Despite barely knowing me, she leaned into me. I hesitantly put my arm around her. She was much older than Abel, but she seemed smaller and more fragile. I hugged her with one arm as she rested her head on my left breast.

I wanted to tell her that her father wasn't a monster, that he was in pain, and that sometimes pain made people look like monsters when they really weren't. But I felt that was something she needed to discover for herself. And if the first thing I tried to talk about was her father, she'd have thrown me out of her bedroom and never let me back in, and never trusted an outsider again.

I let Leila go, stood and walked to her bookshelf where she had little statues of animals that once belonged to a part of the Globe called Africa.

"Abel would love these," I said.

"Who's Abel?" Leila said quietly.

"My son." I turned to face her, smiled, then turned back. "He's just turned five."

"What is he like?"

"Well..." I said. I didn't know where to begin. How do you describe someone when all your feelings and opinions about them revolve around their intangible and invisible essence? "He has dark brown hair and grey eyes, just like my mother's. He's quite tall for his age. I'd say he looks about seven. He's gentle and kind."

"That's boring stuff," Leila said. "Tell me something you wouldn't think to tell a stranger."

She was right. And I thought, what kind of writer am I when I can't even describe my own son? I thought back to last night at home when he tried to sleep in his shoes.

"Okay then. He has a pair of shoes with animals all over them that he never takes off. The animals remind me of yours. They used to live in the jungle in hot countries. Last night he tried to wear his shoes to bed. When I asked why, he told me that they were for protection. I asked what he needed protection against, and he said, "I don't. It's for the animals. I don't want them to get lost in the dark.""

Leila chuckled and nodded with a smile. I heard a spring groan in her mattress and the sound of her feet pattering on the carpet as she approached me from behind. She picked up a little giraffe about the size of my palm, kissed its head, and placed it in my hand.

"That's for Abel, then." Leila stared at me with that same smile she'd had at Anima Cemetery. The one that seemed to mask her pain.

"Thank you," I said. "He'll love it." I kissed its head too. Leila laughed and I put the giraffe in my jacket pocket.

"Have you decided whether you're going to marry a single donor?" I asked. I knew it was a bit of an intrusive question, and rather out of the blue, but children say what they want and mean without sugar-coating anything, so why shouldn't we all?

Leila pursed her lips and shook her head.

"Is that an I-don't-know or an I'm-not-going-to-marry-one?"

"Not going to marry one."

I almost told her she should reconsider, that life would be better that way, more secure, easier, and then I realized how hypocritical it would sound. It would be hard for me to explain, to make sense of it fast enough for her to understand. I hardly understood it myself. I had no idea why I wanted to protect her, and why protecting her meant doing the complete opposite of what I believed in. That moment, I realized that what I believed in was simply my son and what was right in my eyes. I had no idea what I truly believed in at all. I hadn't grown up; I hadn't thought about it seriously enough to have an opinion.

"Okay," I said instead. "I didn't marry mine. Your mother didn't either. You do realize that makes it a harder slog, right?"

"Yes." Leila nodded. "But I don't want to spend my life answering to anyone."

"That's a very grown-up thing to say," I said. A second later I realized that it wasn't grown up at all. It was selfish and irresponsible. She should be thinking about her child. I started to cry. I don't know why, but I'd become so overwhelmed by my realization that my head was flooding with emotion with a pang of regret. Leila blinked as my shoulders shook in silence, standing smack bang in the middle of her bedroom. She didn't say a word until my episode had passed and I had calmed down. When I came up for air, she handed me a tissue, and asked, "Why?"

I didn't know whether she was asking why she sounded grown up or why I was crying. I chose to answer the latter.

"I've just realized how selfish I've been."

"How can you say that? Mum told me you're a tatter and that you do everything to make sure your son is happy."

"I do now, but I didn't then," I said, hardly knowing where I was going with this. Was I trying to manipulate this poor girl into marrying a donor, or was I really actually saying something I believed in? I couldn't trust the words that came out of my own mouth anymore.

"But he wasn't born then," Leila said.

"He *was* born. Somewhere in this universe. And he was destined to exist in the FLP with me when he got here. I should have done more before he was born to make sure he'd be happy. This is no life, this life I have now. I chose to not be dependent on anyone, I chose to take control of my life, but all that meant is that instead I'm dependent on everyone. Without other people, people like your mother, my family wouldn't survive. If I could turn back time, I think I'd have married a single donor, or at least made an effort to find myself someone to love, to share my life with." I looked up then, looked Leila straight in her eyes. "Like your mother did." The words came out effortlessly. If I hadn't been so shocked at what I'd said, I would have been impressed with myself.

Leila scrunched up her nose and flung herself face down on the bed with her arms stretched out to her sides. She looked like a crucifixion that'd fallen over forwards.

"I can find work," she said, her voice muffled by her pillow.

I laughed. "How will you work when your child is a baby and needs you around all the time?"

Leila shrugged. "I don't have to work straight away. I can wait till she's older."

"That's what I did," I said. "But people don't hire single mothers."

"What do you mean?"

"They think they are unreliable."

"That's ridiculous."

"Not in their eyes, it isn't, and while I don't agree, I can understand why. If your child is sick or has an accident at school, you'd have to leave work to collect them. And if there's only you, there's no one to share that responsibility with. And if you're constantly leaving work because of your child, you are deemed unreliable."

Leila tuts and groans. "You're starting to sound like Mum. I thought you were cool, but I guess I was wrong."

"I'm not telling you to marry a donor, Leila."

"What are you telling me then?"

"I'm telling you that Jerome saved your mum from a really tough life, and maybe you should cut him some slack once in a while." That wasn't where I had intended this conversation to lead, but I couldn't stop myself from blurting it out now that it was so obvious.

Leila sat up and ground her teeth. "He's not my father."

I scoffed. "Leila, you don't have to call him Dad to show some respect for him. And maybe if you got to know him as a person, rather than a father, you'd get along."

Leila's nostrils flared. All I'd wanted to do was bond with her, and I ended up giving her a lecture about something I had little knowledge about myself instead. Did I regret it? Yeah, a little. But everything I'd said was instinctual, Eve. I could see that Jerome was a good man, and I truly wanted to help.

"I don't care what kind of person he is," Leila said and crossed her arms. "I hate him. And thanks a lot."

"For what?" I asked.

"For fucking nothing. You can go now." Leila glared at me and pointed her finger toward her door.

WATCH

J erome stared at Leila's half-eaten bowl of fish soup; the potatoes, carrots and broth eaten, and the pieces of fish stuck to the bottom of the dish like chopped up corpses.

Selma rested her hand on his. It lingered there for a few moments, until Jerome's right eye twitched and he stood up, clearing his throat.

"Maybe it wasn't a good idea to bring Icasia here," he said. He started clearing away the dishes one at a time, walking to the sink and back to the table, over and over. Every time he picked up a plate, he made a noise through his nose like he was trying to propel an insect from it.

Selma fell silent. She watched Jerome's movements as he spoke.

"I think she's nice—" Jerome said, after Selma didn't respond.

Selma lifted her elbow onto the back of the chair and rested her head on her fist. She squinted at Jerome and smacked her lips.

"—but, you know, I'm not sure she's going to be a good influence on Leila. She seems too ... how do I put this? Radical? Yes, radical. Leila is going through one of the hardest periods of her life and she needs people around her who are firmly grounded."

Selma tutted. "Why are you always so eclipsed by preconception?"

"What? I am not."

"Yes, you are. You always see the worst in people before you make the effort to get to know them. I know you have high expectations, but the least you could do is show some respect."

"Look. I know you hired her, and I'm sure it was for a good reason, and I'm not going to ask you about your motives because your business is your business, but don't you think she's a bit of a ... how should I put it? Rag doll?"

Selma puckered her brow to the swish and rattle of Jerome rinsing dishes and putting them in the dishwasher. She stood up and pushed her chair under the table. It scraped along the floor, the sound momentarily harmonizing with the hum of the dishwasher starting up.

"Don't forget to wipe the sink down when you're finished," Selma snapped, and headed to the lounge room. She sat on the couch and switched on the inTel.

Images of the Underground flashed on the screen. Beautiful red apples, tomatoes, strawberries, raspberries and cranberries fill one aisle. The next aisle over was packed to the brim with green vegetables, and the one next to that held all the yellow produce—lemons, grapefruit, squash, capsicum, bananas, and corn.

The camera approached a glass-cased pit containing the skeletons of what they'd estimated to be roughly 150 men, women and children thrown in pell-mell, apparently without ceremony or any mark of respect. It paused at the grave and zoomed in close enough to focus on a bronze statuette, around ten inches high, of a standing youth. The index and pinkie fingers of its right hand had been broken and the nose slightly squashed. Its posture seemed graceful, and its large, almond-shaped eyes and dreamy gaze made it look like an athlete.

A news anchor appeared on the screen.

"Though not documented in our archives, there are rumors down here that this grave site, recently uncovered when a new Staller started clearing out his Slot, dated back to 430-420 B.C. and was once part of an archaeological display at Kerameikos subway station. Despite popular opinion that the Underground was once a part of the subway system from London in the United Kingdom—hence its name—we are starting to believe that the land we walk on was once part of a country called Greece."

"What?" Selma whispered, and called Jerome to come in to see.

The anchor continued as Jerome entered and stood by the couch, leaning his hip into the side of the backrest, "We tried to contact Governor Jacobson to confirm these suspicions, but he was unavailable to comment at that time. Speculation and rumors persist among the Stallers down here, and it's a welcome distraction from the latest amendments to the Transition Law. Can you imagine, traveling on a train to go to work, and seeing Greek historical remains as you bought your ticket? Sounds like a dream from the SLP, don't you think?

"On a related matter, it is also rumored that hundreds of letters supporting the legalization of the Underground have reached Governor Jacobson since the Transition Law amendment. We all know that Governor Jacobson tends to ignore public demands over the weekend, so why not all week? It's become a popular opinion that hundreds of people populating enclosed spaces is not actually a risk to public health since it's been happening behind closed doors—no pun intended—for decades now without creating any problems.

On this matter Governor Jacobson did comment. He said, quote, "I'll think about it." Close quote. This is positive news, and rather exciting, since it has been more than 50 years now since any form of public opinion has managed to sway the government."

"No, actually. You know what, Jerome?" Selma said, pointing to the inTel. "She's not a rag doll and she's not a radical. She's just like these people. She's street smart, wise, self-educated, and she knows how to take care of herself, her son and her parents without having a steady job. And she does not conform just because the Book says it's the best route to a happy life. Those kinds of people are the ones who initiate change, Jerome. And I think that's pretty amazing, if you ask me. I think she would be an excellent influence on Leila. She would probably be an excellent influence on you, too." Selma blushed as the sounds of the dishwater groaning and flushing wafted through the door.

Jerome muttered something in response, but Selma couldn't hear it.

"Jome, she may dress a little out there, but ..." Selma paused, "she's an aspiring writer." Selma looked into her lap when her cheeks flushed.

Jerome sat next to Selma on the couch and turned to face her. He smiled as if he was trying to hold in a laugh, his cheeks puffing up a little. He kissed Selma's forehead. He launched into full-blown laughter, flinging his head backwards. "*That*'s why she looks like that! Why didn't you just say so earlier? Here I was stupidly thinking she was going to persuade Leila to live on the streets with a newborn baby."

Selma sighed. "That's ridiculous. If I thought that might be on the cards I wouldn't have fucking invited her over." Selma playfully poked Jerome in the chest. "Hmm, I get why Leila wants to use that word."

Jerome laughed again. "You might want to ask her to give you some lessons on how to use it—"

Selma interrupted, "But seriously Jome, we really need to talk." Selma rested her hand on his knee.

Jerome groaned and let his body fall back into the couch with his arms up and his head resting in his hands. "Not now, Selma. I'm not in the mood to talk about it."

"But we have to. We need to make a plan before it's too late."

"You mean *you* need to make a plan."

Selma pulled Jerome's hands away from his head and turned his face to make eye contact with her. She looked his tall and thin, but masculine, body up and down, his big brown eyes and floppy mop of a fringe. Tears welled up in her eyes. "Jome, I—"

Selma stopped short as she heard Leila's bedroom door open and close. Icasia's shoes squeaked as she strode across the kitchen floor.

Selma and Jerome looked up with friendly smiles as she approached the couch. Icasia took a deep breath and held it for a moment. As she exhaled, she said, "Could I bring Abel next time? Leila says she'd like to meet him."

Selma glanced momentarily at Jerome then turned to look at Icasia. Icasia's question lingered in the air like the hum of fingertips caressing the rims of crystal glasses.

"I think that's a lovely idea," Selma said. "And you're both welcome in our home any time. It was a pleasure having you here tonight." Selma turned to face Jerome, whose eyes were locked on Icasia's tattoos. "Isn't that right, Jerome? We'd love to have them both visit." Selma widened her eyes.

"Um ... yeah, of course," Jerome stammered. "A pleasure."

For a moment the expression on his face looked as though

he'd swallowed a fly. Selma subtly elbowed him in his side. He buckled a little and pretended to cough.

"Icasia," Jerome said with a smirk. "Would you like a cup of Joe to wash down the fish?"

LISTEN

E ve, you have no idea how repulsed I was by the combination of coffee and fish—which I'm sure was Jerome's intention—but I accepted his offer and sat on the armchair opposite the couch.

Something was up. I could tell by the look on Selma's face. I'd never seen her smile look forced before, but it did then. I knew that now wasn't the right time to pry, not if I was to become acquainted and make sure Jerome felt comfortable having me around. I figured something must have gone on while I was in Leila's bedroom, but for all I knew it was unrelated to me, so I just went with the flow and tried to ignore Selma's apparent discomfort.

Jerome handed me a mug with a bluebird on it. It caught me by surprise. In tiny letters along the inside of the handle, it read *Anima Cemetery*.

I frowned. Jerome laughed.

"Every time we visit, they give us another one. Might as well use them."

I raised my eyebrows, wondering why anyone would want to drink out of something that reminded them of death. And who in Jacobson's name had thought of producing Anima Cemetery commemorative mugs?

"I know. It's pretty stupid," Jerome said, and sat next to Selma again, who couldn't stop fidgeting.

"So, Selma tells me you're a writer?"

I slurped my coffee and nodded. "Aspiring," I said, to make sure it was clear that I hadn't published anything yet. I didn't want him to think I was an expert and have him expect me to know everything.

"That's interesting. I've always wondered how writers make a living. Now I get why you needed the job at the bakery."

"Oh, I don't work at the bakery. I'm a tatter."

Selma's face went white as Jerome shot a confused look at her, then back at me.

My organs freaked out so hard that my insides felt like they were pieces of orange being sucked off its rind.

I burst into laughter, trying really hard to think of an excuse that would save Selma's ass and not make me look like a complete idiot. "Sorry, ha! I mean, I don't earn a wage. Selma pays me with goods." That really was a close call.

"Selma!" Jerome flicks his head in her direction and flashes her a melodramatic stare. "How can you not pay the poor girl? That's not like you at all."

Selma was about to butt in, but I got in first.

"Oh, I insisted. I'm the one who asked for the job. She wasn't looking for me. And I figured she wouldn't really have a big enough customer base yet to be able to afford it."

Jerome puffed. His lips vibrated. "Sounds like a dud deal to me."

Selma tutted and whacked him on the back of the head. "Thanks a lot, Jome."

He cried out in fake pain and chuckled. "Whatever floats your boat," he said, nodding once in my direction. "An-y-way." Jerome uttered each syllable between diminishing bursts of laughter and then cleared his throat. "I'm intrigued about your writing," he said, suddenly becoming very serious. He reached under the couch, and tugged something off a piece of Velcro. For a moment I thought he was one of those hermit psychopaths I'd heard about on inTel and was pulling a weapon on me. Okay, given my first impression of him that was maybe a bit of an exaggeration, but when I saw the little box of Montecristo cigars, I stopped holding my breath. I didn't want to talk about my writing I wanted to know where the flip he scored those things!

Of course, I didn't ask.

Jerome lit a cigar. His scruffy brown hair fell over his droopy brown eyes. He took a drag, rolled the smoke around his mouth, looked at the cigar as if it was the greatest invention in the Globe, sank back into the couch, sighed and ran a hand through his fringe. I must have waited way too long to answer Jerome's question because he said, "Well, don't let me hold you up," with quite a charming smile on his face. Selma looked at him with such awe. He winked at her and patted her thigh. With Leila out of the room, they had loosened up.

"Well, I'm trying to write a book called *The Pros and Cons of Living Beyond the Book*," I said, holding tightly onto my mug. I looked into my lap, then at Selma, to check if it was okay to continue. She barely nodded at me, but it *was* a nod. "I need to research some real cases, though," I said. "Clearly I can't just base it on my own experiences. That would be biased."

Jerome took another drag of his cigar and hmm-ed as though he were genuinely interested. Well, shit. I was genuinely interested myself, and started to wonder whether I should actually try to write the book. Taking a serious interest in the information I would gather would probably help me choose a direction for my own life.

I needed more. And I needed to learn how to do it without

plotting the things I could get in return. This need I felt, there in Selma's armchair, after witnessing the signs of love between two people not bound by blood, shook me up.

I made a decision there and then. I would write this book.

"Selma said she wouldn't be opposed to me gathering some information from her, and I have been, but I'd really appreciate your cooperation as well, if you feel comfortable with that, of course." I startled myself with my professional yet sympathetic tone. I'd mimicked exactly the way the anchors talked on inTel when conducting interviews. My confidence rose.

Jerome sat up and rested his elbows on his thighs, letting his hands hang between his knees. The cigar smoke wafted into the air, swirling over his face like a rising soul.

He squinted and licked his lips. For a split second he seemed skeptical. Paranoia had gotten the better of me.

"I bet you're wondering where I got these cigars," he said.

"Jome," Selma purred, "that's not answering Icasia's question."

Jerome maintained a solid stare in my direction. "Patience, Sma. I'll get to that."

He nodded at me as a request to answer.

"I am, actually. It was the first thing I thought when I realized you weren't pulling out a weapon."

"Well—" Jerome laughed, coughed, and with a touch of pride in his voice, he said, "I have a mate whose ancestors originated from a place called Greece, way back before the Movement."

"I know about Greece," I said, eager to show off. "I've read all about how Germany and the USA conspired to bankrupt the country so that they were unable to engage in export and import to support their economy. Citizens' bank accounts were wiped clean to pay off a supposed debt, and they were pretty much left to scavenge the streets for leftovers."

"Good. That will make my explanation easier."

Intrigued, I leaned forward, cupping my mug in both hands.

"When Greece could no longer support itself as an independent country, Germany and the USA basically claimed it as their own. This marked the absolute beginning of the Jacobson Movement when the very first Jacobson, Helga Smith Jacobson, was elected into government. At that time my mate's great great *great* grandfather got a hold of something like a hundred million boxes of elite cigars from a Nigerian guy who was selling stolen goods to support his family. A few years later, when the Jacobson Movement started gaining momentum, but before it claimed every country on the planet and molded it into one united federation, they started to package everything into the unlabeled airtight plastic boxes we know today, and this man helped hide them in an abandoned fallout shelter. You know what that is?"

I nodded, still not quite sure where Jerome's story was going.

"Right, well. He told no one except his children, and his children told their children, and their children told their children."

"Jerome," Selma whispered. "Are you sure you want to reveal this stuff?"

Jerome shrugged. "Got less than six months to live anyway. What're they gonna do? Kill me?"

Selma closed her eyes and gritted her teeth. She turned her head as her eyes grew moist.

"Anyway. The tradition was passed down from generation to generation and the family sold them to earn a living. All my mate needs to do is sell one packet a day and he makes enough Sats to survive. Obviously, he sells more than one packet a day. He's pretty much raking it in, and has helped us out on many an occasion."

"Okay," I said, noticing Selma wince. "But I feel like I'm missing the point."

"That's because I haven't got to it yet." Jerome laughed and Selma forced a smile while pretending to nudge something out of her eye to avoid the tears. "My mate doesn't live by the Book. He is wifeless, childless, and has never even donated to Prems because he's always shot blanks." Jerome scoffed. "Poor guy. Probably smoked too much. Anyway. He asked me to follow on the tradition. He's still got around two hundred thousand boxes left."

Selma shifts in her seat. "You never told me that, Jome."

"I didn't tell you because I didn't accept it. But I know he'll be around for a lot longer than me."

Selma rolled her eyes, probably at yet another mention of his life span.

"Anyway. My point is, if there is anyone who understands what it's like to not live by the Book, it's my mate Hector. I'll get you in touch."

I laugh. "You could've just told me that you had a mate I could talk to in the first place."

Jerome smiled and dropped his cigar in his empty coffee cup, where it hissed briefly. "If I'd've just told you that, you wouldn't be as intrigued as you are now and you would have insisted on still speaking to me."

"Oh," I said. "You don't want to contribute to my research?"

"Nope." Jerome stroked another tear from Selma's cheek. She didn't try to hide it this time. "My soul is my own, and only my own."

I didn't go back to Selma's for dinner for at least a month. And when I did visit, Jerome was out. All the time, Eve. *All the time.* Selma and I racked our brains each morning over coffee and cake for ways we could get through to him. "He refuses to listen to me. He refuses to open up," she would say over and over. Every morning. Every hour.

The morning after Jerome's first DeathCare Therapy session was the worst I'd seen Selma. We didn't talk. I just watched her bake, leaning against the kitchen counter, listening to her crying and going on and on about Jerome's stubbornness and irresponsibility and the impenetrable establishment. I asked for us to sit down and try to relax. But she said she needed to stay occupied, otherwise she'd probably get herself killed by going to Anima Cemetery and doing something she'd regret.

Selma told me that the night of Jerome's first DeathCare Therapy session, he came home mute. He locked himself in the bathroom. And threw up. For three hours straight. By the time he surfaced, Selma said he looked green. She tried to talk about what had happened during the session to cause him so much anxiety. But he wouldn't talk.

DEATHCARE SESSION 1, NEURAL OSCILLATION REGISTRY NO. 9781925965605

Jerome stared at the clean vertical scar running down the center of his DeathCare therapist's forehead as he escorted him into his office. He wondered if his therapist's brain had been replaced with one of the AlterChips he helped manufacture at work for a stand-by Global military team. The therapist's sky-blue suit shone under the fake, blue-tinged sunbeams that radiated from the digital skylight. Jerome glanced at the floor as he approached the couch. It was cloudy outside. His feet were placed firmly on the ground, or at least the floor, but he couldn't see them touching anything but air.

He recalled the first time he walked into a government setting like this. He'd had to grab onto something to catch his balance. The closest thing to him was a receptionist. He'd pulled her skirt down by accident.

"Do people really relax in here?" Jerome asked, as he sat opposite the therapist who looked a lot like he could be his brother.

"We're not here to talk about other people, Mr. Bcyett. We're here to talk about you."

"Way to make me feel comfortable, mate. Sideswipe the very first thing I say to you."

The therapist pursed his lips and ran his tongue along his teeth. "If you don't mind, please call me Phyvwonoh instead of mate. It sounds like you're asking me to engage in sexual intercourse." Phyvwonoh snorted at his own joke. Jerome stared and sniffed.

Jerome is going to be a hard case. Sunken shoulders, scraggly hair, misty eyes. Hands in his pockets, fiddling with something inside. Both of them. No rattle. It is probably cotton. He is probably sticking the threads underneath his fingernails. A sure sign of general dissatisfaction. The best way to work this case is to make him feel like he is in control. Emotional manipulation. Reverse psychology.

"I guess you can hear my thoughts like all the other blue suits?" Jerome scoffed. "Won't have to do much talking. Right, Phy?"

Phyvwonoh rubbed a sweaty palm over his knee. Jerome homed in on it and chuckled. Phyvwonoh was new, and Jerome had cottoned on.

Not a good start, thought Phyvwonoh. *According to rule S3.709, allowing the patient to see a therapist's vulnerabilities is tempting failure. But I may be able to find a way into this man's soul, regardless of how I perceived him. He is clearly a 'snail,' as us DCTs like to call them—fragile within, carrying a protective shell wherever they go.*

"Mr. Beyett." Phyvwonoh squinted and licked his lips. "No, actually. I cannot hear your thoughts like all the other blue suits." He winked and wiggled his head side to side trying to lighten the mood. "If DeathCare Therapists were able to hear their patients' thoughts, they would be able to manipulate their free will, and the possibility of influencing their natural thought processes would therefore be very high."

Jerome nodded. Slowly. As if he was beginning to understand.

Phyvwonoh sighed. *Perhaps it won't be so tough after all.* "Our sessions, however, along with both your thoughts and mine, are recorded and registered in the system for future reference should we need to use them for research on how to improve treatment."

"So, what you're saying is—" Jerome said, scratching his head, then leaning forward to rest his elbows on his knees. "This is all an experiment and a scam."

Phyvwonoh's breath caught in his throat. "No, Mr.—"

Jerome held up his hand to signify that he shouldn't interrupt. "And you do as little as possible to actually help us transition into the SLP. Am I right, Phy?"

"No, that's not what I'm saying at all, Mr. Beyett. If you took a moment to better comprehend what I'm saying—"

"To better comprehend? I'm the Co-Head of Robotics at the University of Area 7, and you think I might have trouble understanding you?"

"Mr. Beyett, if you'd just give me a moment to explain that if we were to manipulate your thought processes, then the choices you were to make would not be truly yours. You cannot feel happiness by being told you're going to feel it."

Jerome stared and clicked his tongue. Phy was right. Jerome knew it. But he was damned if he was going to let him know he knew it. He wasn't going to leave this place until he told this ... this replicant, or this programmed human, whatever Phyvwonoh was, exactly what he thought of Governor Jacobson and his army of bloody blue beetles.

Jerome thought back to the previous night, when Leila screamed, for the umpteenth time, "You're not my fucking father." It was a great word. *Fuck.* He didn't understand why people hardly used it anymore. He wanted to use it now. It was perfect for everything. You could use it to express so many wonderful feelings ...

"I don't give a fuck anyway. Nothing is going to change in here, Phy."

"Why do you feel nothing is going to change, Mr. Beyett?"

Jerome laughed and sarcastically whacked his hand on his forehead. "Because it's too late! I can't change my ways in less than six months, and I think you know that better than I do. Don't you, Phy? This—this *stuff*. It's all show. You're showing the Globe that you are doing something to protect us. That you work for the people. That's the biggest load of fuck I've ever heard in my entire life. If you worked for the fucking people, you would have made more room for us. Not fucking kill us off, you fucking fucked up little blue fucker!"

Phyvwonoh's jaw dropped. *During my year of employment at the DCT Center, I have never encountered one single person who wasn't willing to co-operate. Everybody wants to live. Everybody wants to give their parents a chance to transition. Every child owes their parents at least that. It is their duty.*

"And while I'm enjoying the sound of my own voice, because it's quite rare for me to raise it like this and I think it's quite becoming—don't you?—let me ask you something."

Phyvwonoh raised his eyebrows, closed his mouth and involuntarily held his breath.

"Why *blue*? It's the color of depression, you fuckwit. Do you want everyone to fucking die while you tell them you want the opposite? Is it some sort of subliminal trigger? I mean, what's your DeathCare Therapy success rate? I'd like to know how many people Governor Jacobson has saved, you motherfucker." Jerome stopped and took a deep breath. He was about to continue when he realized he'd forgotten his next question. "Argh ... fuck it. Fuck *you*, Phy. Fuck *all* of you," Jerome barked, concluding the last sentence by sticking up his middle finger in front of Phyvwonoh's face.

Rule S4.607: Ignore all outbursts of dissatisfaction and attempts at revolt against the government. Patients are under a lot of pressure and should be expected to misbehave. If the behavior continues in the same manner after one month, then the assigned therapist has the right to transfer the patient to another therapist. A patient may be reassigned only once. It is the therapist's responsibility to lead the patient in the right direction. If the patient fails to find happiness by their due date, then their assigned therapist will be forced to resign.

Phyvwonoh looked down into the clouds for a moment and breathed slowly and quietly through his nose and out of his mouth. *I have not failed one patient yet and I don't intend Jerome Beyett to be my first. I can't afford to lose my job. It's everything I have worked toward. And I need the perks. I need to maintain the ability to bypass the Transition Grave and move into the SLP when I retire. If I lose my job, my benefits will go out the window and I'll be just like everyone else.*

Jerome plonked himself down, lengthways on the couch. "Okay, Phy. Hit me with your best stuff."

"Mr. Beyett," Phyvwonoh whispered. He felt for his pulse. *It's a little quick, but nothing to be alarmed about. Stay calm and take the job in your stride. You cannot control other people's actions, but you can guide them toward making better choices.*

"I am going to address all your questions today," Phyvwonoh said with a sigh. "Because I would like to facilitate your peace of mind before we move forward—"

"Fuck my peace of mind," Jerome muttered under his breath.

"One. Yoo, you can change your ways in less than six

months. In fact, 89% of urgent cases are successful within the first four, which is how much time *you* have left, Mr. Beyett. The other 11%, unfortunately, are people who don't trust the system. If you can find a way to trust the system, Mr. Beyett, I think you and I will do very well here.

"Two. Governor Jacobson *did* create more space for us. Governor Jacobson *created* the SLP. I'm sure you know that, Mr. Beyett. It is common knowledge. However, as I'm also sure you know, the SLP is supposed to be a place of eternal peace and pleasure. And if it is filled with people who do not already know how that feels, it will just turn into another Globe. And that wouldn't be any good for anybody. And we wouldn't want that, would we Mr. Beyett?

"Three. Why blue? It represents tranquility, promoting both physical and mental relaxation. Blue represents reliability and responsibility, inner security and confidence. And above all, blue is the color of trust, honesty, and loyalty. Now, have I addressed all your questions, Mr. Beyett? May we begin what you have come here for?"

Phyvwonoh smiled. *You have asserted yourself in this difficult situation without losing your temper or compromising the task at hand. You must pat yourself on the back.*

"Will you now give me my due respect, and realize that we both want the same thing: for you to find happiness. For your parents to transition into the SLP. To wait with Selma, your love, for Leila to gift you with more life."

Jerome sat up, stood, walked toward Phyvwonoh and snatched his Quill from behind his ear with a wink that imitated the one Phyvwonoh had offered him earlier. He wrote on Phyvwonoh's forehead: *FUCKING BULLSHIT.*

LISTEN

Selma had been scrubbing the inside of her clean oven for over half an hour before I knelt down, reached inside, took hold of her hand, and pried the scourer from it.

"You need to stop," I said. I threw the scourer into the sink from where I was kneeling on the cold hard floor. And Eve, it was a *very* cold hard floor. I was desperate to stand up.

Selma covered her face with her hands, screamed into them, smearing soapy grime down her cheeks.

"Why the total sarcastic attitude about his life? Is all I can do now to hope Phyvwonoh gets through to him?"

"The way I see it," I said, "You have two choices. One: you can put all your faith in Phyvwonoh and risk Jerome's soul being annihilated and regret forever the fact that you didn't try to help him when you might have been able to. Or two: try every possible solution you can to save Jerome despite the fact that it is possibly destroying your marriage. You'll just have to hope you can pull through it."

"Neither of those options sound good to me."

"Selma—"

"I think I'm just going to have to accept his fate. Jerome's soul is going to be annihilated. In four months' time he'll be gone and I'm never going to see him again."

"Don't be ridiculous. You're letting this get the better

of you," I said, taking hold of Selma's shoulders. "You're stronger than this, I know it. And I think you know it too. You're just feeling overwhelmed. I mean, I know I would be too, but you're a smart woman. I knew that the moment I entered this bakery and first met you. You'll find a way through this, I know it." I know that as pep talks go it was pretty lame, Eve, but I had to say something. I hadn't got the hang of this friendship thing yet, but something was beginning to click. It seemed that no matter what I said, Selma still responded as if I was being helpful. I didn't really understand why, but I eventually realized that sometimes you just need someone there, whether they say anything or not. And when they do say something, it doesn't make a difference, because you're *there*. Just *there*. Do you ever feel like that, Eve? I know I do.

"I think Jerome is stronger than me, Icasia," Selma said. "He's the one who's on death row, and I'm the one who's breaking down."

"He's not stronger, Selma. If he was, he'd get the fuck over himself and let everyone try to help him. And he'd stop being so selfish."

Selma pressed her lips together.

"He is being selfish, isn't he? It's not just me being insensitive?"

"If anyone can recognize selfish, it's me." I scoffed. "And look. I know that time seems very short, but Phyvwonoh said the chances of success are high."

"Only if Jerome decides to cooperate." Selma gave me a lopsided smile and stood up. She held out her hand to help me up. "You should get home to Abel. I'll be all right here. I've cried enough."

"Abel is with my parents. He's used to being without me until the evening, so don't you worry about him."

I touched Selma's cheek gently and said, "What do you need? I'll do it for you." We held each other's gaze. Selma's moist hazel eyes reflected flecks of blue and green in the sunlight that streamed in through the slits in the blinds in the kitchen. Her breath steadied and slowed as she placed her right hand over my heart. I rested my other hand over hers, squeezed it and winked.

"You're very beautiful, do you know that?" Selma said, tilting her head to the side and staring into my eyes. She squinted, smiled, and expelled a tiny puff of air from her nose as if she'd just understood something.

I blushed and stepped backward slightly. "Thanks," I said, trying to sound more grateful than embarrassed. I had no idea what that was, but it didn't just feel like a friendly compliment. No one had ever said anything like that to me before. I had no idea what the etiquette was. Was I meant to say it back? Was I supposed to find something else about the other person to flatter them with?

Selma chuckled and grabbed a tea towel. "Unfortunately," she said, whacking the counter with it, "your beauty is not going to help my family, is it?"

I frowned. Something sparked in my mind. I thought for a moment, as Selma wiped her hands dry and went out front. I followed a few steps behind.

"Selma?"

"Hmm?" Selma hummed as she grabbed a couple of blue glass bottles of sparkling water.

We reached the table and sat down. Selma opened a bottle and slid it across to me. I caught it without looking.

"It might," I said, as I pulled my chair in and swigged my bubbles.

"What might what?"

"Beauty might actually help your family."

"Excuse me?" I didn't know what was going through her head, but judging by the look on her face I think she was on the verge of being offended.

"Selma, can you keep an open mind for a moment?" I flattened my hands on the table, like she often did, to show I was serious. "Just listen to what I have to say—objectively—without getting upset, okay?"

Selma sat back, crossed her arms and legs, and said after a few moments pause, "How can I promise not to get upset if you think what you say might upset me?"

She had a point, Eve. But it didn't stop me from voicing my opinion. What did I really have to lose, Eve? If she threw me out, I had enough skills to tit-for-tat elsewhere. The only thing that made me hesitate was the possibility of jeopardizing our relationship. For the first time in my life, such a thought gave me a hollow feeling in my stomach. It bothered me. Nothing like this had ever bothered me before, and the feeling caught me by surprise. But I had to rationalize this if I truly thought that what I was about to say would save Jerome. I took a deep breath, closed my eyes, and blurted it out despite not knowing how to word it tactfully.

"What if—if Jerome feels—uh, you know ... trapped?" I stammered. "You know, in a relationship sense?"

"Icasia ..." Selma scraped her bottom teeth over her top lip and squinted at me. "I don't follow."

"What if he needs to ... have an affair?"

Selma glared as her cheeks grew red. I immediately regretted it. What did I know about having an affair and the feelings associated with it, other than what I'd read at the library? The tendons in her neck flexed. I thought she was going to yell and scream and tell me to get out and never come back. But instead, she burst into tears again, tangling her fingers into her hair.

"Oh bliss!" Selma cried, flinging her head back. "You think?"

I shrugged. I was almost certain, but I needed to lighten the load a little by expressing some doubt. "I'm just speculating, because I think you need to explore all possibilities. I'm thinking that maybe he's dissatisfied with his life and I don't think it has to do with his job. Maybe it's, you know, some kind of mid-life crisis."

Selma shook her head. "No, that's impossible. People don't go through that sort of crap anymore. Do they?"

"I don't know. Do you?"

Selma's eyes widened. "No. I don't."

I frowned with concern. For real. I was genuinely feeling compassionate, and it gave me hope.

"No. You're wrong," Selma said, shaking her head. "That *can't* be the problem."

"How can you be so sure?"

"Because love doesn't trigger happiness, Icasia. Success does. Love hurts, remember?"

"But what if they've got it wrong?" I said. I wasn't really that sure about what I was saying, but I never understood the rules, or how things like that worked, so I naturally thought outside the box. "What if it's not really success that triggers happiness?"

"How do you mean?"

"Well, couldn't it be a combination of things? Take you and this bakery for instance," I said, shifting in my seat a little. "You told me yourself that you'd already baked a lot at home, and that you hadn't worked since marrying Jerome. And maybe being stuck at home wasn't good enough for you."

"So?"

"Don't you think it shows you're more fulfilled than successful? I mean, it was never your ambition to open a bakery, and you'd already found a sense of happiness from baking at home. But it wasn't until you opened the bakery that you got the Letter."

"I know that, Icasia. But I still don't understand how that's relevant to Jerome needing to have an affair."

I groaned in frustration. It was so clear in my head, but I couldn't articulate it properly. "Because you filled a gap in your life by opening the bakery, Selma!" I said, whacking the edge of the table with my hand. Selma jolted in her seat. "You never *dreamed* of opening a bakery, you never strived for *any* kind of success, but when you did, you finally had a reason to get out of the house and do something with a skill you enjoyed. Can't you see? You completed the picture. And I don't think that picture would have been completed if you'd opened a bakery without having Leila and Jerome in your life too. I think you needed all of those things for it to happen. It filled the last hole."

Selma stared at the tabletop and wiped her eyes dry.

"Please tell me that I'm making sense," I said. "Because I'm raising my voice and I don't know why. I've never done that before, and I'm sorry."

"You think Jerome's last hole is sex?" Selma said, ignoring my apology. I didn't blame her. It was a lot to take in. It was a lot for *me* to take in. All these ideas weren't things I'd been thinking about. They had flooded in unannounced when Selma told me I was beautiful and made my stomach do a back flip at the slight sense of belonging and need I'd felt.

"I can't say for sure," I said. "But I read in the archives recently that sex used to be the first thing men thought about when they woke up. That's biological need, Selma. It really can't be any different now, no matter how much we ignore it."

Selma laughed, forcing more tears to stream down her cheeks. "We haven't made love in over a year."

I smiled. I knew I was onto something.

"Icasia, if you're right, I'm going to have to ask Jerome to sleep with another woman, aren't I?"

I pressed my lips together and nodded.

"And if you're wrong, I'll have asked my husband to sleep with another woman for nothing, won't I?"

I touched my hand to my forehead as if I had a fever. I was hot and flushed and stressing out at the idea of ruining the only proper relationship outside my family I'd possibly ever have. Despite believing every word I said, I had doubts about whether it would work. But you can't blame me, can you, Eve? I mean, I could feel it in my bones—something wasn't right about what the Book said our purpose was. And there's no denying that a man's sexual instincts were still thriving, even in a world like this. They may have been suppressed and controlled, but there was no way they had ceased to exist. And I was positive there had to be something more to finding happiness than having a successful career.

"Maybe you can try and suss it out of him," I said. "Without actually asking him point blank? Make it seem like it's *his* idea."

"How do you suggest I do that? He is the most loyal person I know."

"I don't know ... uh ... try to make love to him when he really isn't in the mood, and when he rejects you, you could accuse him of not finding you attractive anymore." Eve, I tell you, I had no idea where I was coming up with these ideas, and I was convincing myself more and more every day that I should pursue writing for real.

Selma groaned. "That's ... that's manipulation."

"You're not exactly pure anymore, Selma," I said. "Don't forget you lied about my motives for being in your house."

Selma looked into her lap. After a short pause, she said, "Doing something like that is bound to lead to an argument, I'm sure."

"Exactly. And that would give you the opportunity to suggest he have an affair. But you have to wait until he admits he thinks about other women. Okay?"

"And what if he denies ever thinking about those things?"

"Selma. He's a man. What man of any age would refuse that kind of freedom and opportunity?"

Selma shook her head and hung it in her hands. "Okay," she said, grabbing both my hands. "I'll do it tonight."

Eve. I panicked.

What was I doing?

Yes, she had asked for my help, but was this really the solution?

My doubt grew and grew and haunted me every night until ... well, you'll soon see.

WATCH

Selma bit her thumbnail as she watched Jerome scraping the scraps off the dinner plates into the garbage with a fork.

Jerome spun around and put his hands in his pockets before leaning his hip on the counter. He stared at Selma. His eyes were empty—soulless and blank—prepared for death.

Death.

Not a word commonly used outside DeathCare.

People don't often *die*. They transition.

Death is a word associated with failure.

Failure to connect with your true inner self.

"I'm a failed human on death row," Jerome said, his nostrils flaring.

Selma stepped forward and cupped Jerome's face, stroked her thumb along his cheek bone, her middle finger hooked behind his ear. She pulled his head toward hers and kissed his top lip, slipping her tongue inside his mouth. But her tongue met a firm wall of teeth. She whispered, "Please," and forced her tongue in his mouth.

For a moment Jerome gave in and parted his lips. Selma's tongue slid along his own as he remained leaning on the counter, hands in pockets, the rest of his body unresponsive.

Selma ran her hands down his back and pulled his pelvis closer to hers. She took his hands and held them against her breasts. "Make love to me," she whispered.

A brief groan of pleasure escaped Jerome's lips. Selma reciprocated with a similar sound ... until he pushed her off.

"Not now, Sma. This isn't the time."

Selma straightened her top.

"And when exactly is it the time, Jerome?"

"Here we go," Jerome grumbled. He glared at her and puffed. "We all know what happens when you use my full name, don't we? There's always an aftermath when I don't do exactly what you want. Why do you always need so much, and complain that you never get it even when you do?" Jerome almost spat as he spoke.

Selma stepped back and crossed her arms. "Uh ... excuse me?"

"A few minutes in the missionary is not going to help anything." Jerome's voice lowered in volume as if he'd regretted his outburst.

"How dare you?" Selma hissed. "I have done nothing to deserve this. All I'm doing is trying to love you."

"Do I need you to show me that I've failed as a lover too?"

"Jerome!" Selma's jaw dropped. "What has gotten into you? Since when are we not on the same team? Time is running out. Do want to spend it miserable or happy?"

Jerome laughed. "Miserable or happy? Have you forgotten why we are having this argument in the first place?"

Selma pressed her right eyebrow with two forefingers. "I'm sorry. Bad choice of words."

Jerome stared at his shoes.

"I can't fuck a memory. If you're not going to do anything to help yourself live, the least you can do is *love* me. Make love to me. I *need* you."

Selma started to cry. Jerome stepped forward and took her in his arms. He held her tight and rocked her back and forth, kissing her head and whispering, "I do love you. I love you. Very much."

"Then why won't you make love to me?"

"I am just not in the mood, Sma. I have a lot on my mind. It's not a reflection of how I feel for you. You *know* I love you. Please trust me."

"You don't find me attractive anymore, do you?" Selma stepped back, gulped and crossed her arms under her breasts.

"What?" Jerome craned his neck. "Don't be ridiculous."

"We haven't made love in over a year, Jome."

"That's irrelevant. We've had a busy year. You said yourself that starting the bakery was taking up all your time."

"I'm not there at night, Jome. I'm not there when we're in bed."

Jerome pinched the bridge of his nose.

"Are you having an affair?" Selma sucked in her bottom lip as it shuddered.

Jerome scoffed. "Do you really think I'm capable?"

Selma's lips parted to speak multiple times before she simply said, "Yes, I do."

Jerome's shoulders drooped.

"I'm not, Sma. And you know what? I'm really disappointed that you think I could do such a thing after all these years of mutual trust."

Selma swallowed and glanced at her feet. "I wouldn't be disappointed if you had," Selma whispered. "I would think—" Selma coughed to hide the wavering in her voice, "I'd think it only natural for you to want to have sexual relations with another woman." She looked Jerome right in the eye and put her hands in her pockets to hide the shaking.

The lines in Jerome's forehead looked like a satellite view of rivers. He frowned at Selma and his eyes filled with tears.

"When we got married, you made it extremely clear that you wouldn't accept anything less than a fully monogamous relationship. Remember? You told me that if I couldn't commit to that, you'd rather transition alone?

Selma gulped.

"There is no reason why I shouldn't be true to my word."

"Well," Selma shrugged. "There should be." Selma's eye twitched and she glanced at her feet to hide it. "I think you should try it."

"Try what?" Jerome's voice raised an octave.

"Having an affair. I think you should sleep with another woman." Selma looked up and burst into tears.

Jerome pulled Selma closer to his body and wiped her tears away with his thumbs. "Why?" he whispered. "What aren't you telling me?"

Selma's breath caught in her throat. She held it there, as if the air was trapped in her lungs.

Because ..." she hesitated, "because I think you need some practice with someone you don't love. Someone you just want to *fuck* and not give damn if you never see them again." The expression on Selma's face took on a personality that didn't belong. The stiffness in her stance relaxed, her body and spirit morphing into the skin of an unknown woman. "I have never had an orgasm with you, Jerome." Selma breathed in a jagged breath as the words echoed in the room. "Not once. I faked them all."

Jerome flinched. His eyes glazed over as he put his hands in his pockets and stepped a few feet backward.

"No," he said. "And that's the last I'm going to say about it."

Selma burst into tears and ran into Jerome's embrace. She

muttered something into his chest in between sobs. A bluebird appeared outside the kitchen window and landed on
the exterior sill. It whistled the tune:

DEATHCARE SESSION 14, NEURAL OSCILLATION REGISTRY NO. 9781925965605

No new words were going to make a difference to what had now come between Jerome and Selma—they would just be letters that strung sounds together. The determination in Selma's voice the previous night clearly showed that she knew what she wanted. So why not? Why not find some stupid single young mother in a bar and screw her brains out? It's been so long since he'd even masturbated. And now that he came to think of it, Selma hadn't been helping either. With her bakery and her indestructible relationship with Icasia, he'd been left out of everything—visibly invisible.

He was alone.

Always had been.

Always would be.

He would do it.

He would tell his wife that if he went through with it to expect him to fall in love with her, to expect their marriage to be over. Absolutely. He could go on some sex rampage and have the time of his life. What did he have to lose? Love is lost when the soul is lost, so what's the fucking difference?

Phyvwonoh released his iNote and Quill into his lap and

pressed his lips together. Every time he contorted his mouth in some way, the holographic clouds below their feet shifted and sighed and the room oozed disappointment and gloom. Jerome groaned at the knowledge that he was the catalyst.

"It's been two weeks," Phyvwonoh said, "and the only remark of possible substance that has emerged from your stubborn lips is that you hate feeling trapped. But I'm afraid I cannot determine how to apply that to your career if you don't expand on it, Jerome. What is it about your job that makes you feel trapped? I need more details."

It's not the job, thought Jerome, its life, it's the Globe, it's bloody Phy. The situation he's in. The tension at home between him and his wife—and daughter—and that fucking wannabe writer.

"Phy, it's hopeless. Can't you just write me off as a dud conception? All this therapy bullshit isn't going to get me— *us*—anywhere. There has to be another way. Isn't there another service you can refer me to, or something? I don't know ... something like LoserCare?" Jerome laughed until he saw the sorrow in Phyvwonoh's expression. He was certain his eyes had glazed over.

For a moment Jerome pitied Phyvwonoh. This was his livelihood. His life. And Jerome's failure could very well be Phyvwonoh's failure too. The people he was going to let down by his forthcoming non-existence kept piling up.

Phyvwonoh stood and then sat next to Jerome. He slipped his Quill behind his ear with his left hand and clutched his iNote to his chest with his right. He rested his left hand on Jerome's knee to stop it from bouncing up and down.

"Relax," Phyvwonoh said, closing his eyes and extending the sibilant at the end of the word. "Imagine you are in your lab. Right this minute. You've just discovered a solution to a manufacturing problem that has been bothering you and many other colleagues for months. Now imagine that finding this solution is the very event that results in you receiving the Letter. Tell me, do you celebrate? How does it make you feel?"

Jerome sighed. In such a situation he decided he would feel relieved. But not for himself. For his mother and father. For Selma. For Phyvwonoh. He didn't give a shit about the job or the Letter. What he gave a shit about was the fact that he wouldn't be responsible for other peoples' pain.

"I've made breakthroughs at work plenty of times in the past," Jerome said, removing Phyvwonoh's hand from his leg. "None of them resulted in the Letter. My job doesn't give me satisfaction. It puts food on the table. As you know, I'm not my wife's assigned donor, so we can't rely on government support. That's all my job is to me. Life support."

Phyvwonoh frowned at Jerome's last statement and rubbed his back as though he were a baby needing to burp. Jerome shrugged Phyvwonoh's hands off and laughed.

"Phy. What are you doing?"

Phyvwonoh stopped and put his hands in his lap. "I apologize. I was lost in thought. At home I comfort my child when I think," he said, looking down at his knees.

Jerome scrutinized the man's wrinkle-free complexion and thin patches of stubble. He couldn't be much older than nineteen or twenty. He was getting career advice from a man who'd hardly had a chance to grow. He'd probably married the woman who was impregnated with his sperm. So, it would be a loveless marriage, no doubt. Regimented. Legal. By the Book.

Before starting these sessions, he'd signed a form which declared he wouldn't ask the therapist any personal questions. He wasn't sure if a penalty existed as he couldn't be bothered reading the form properly, but what was the worst that could happen? That his sessions got terminated? That he got assigned another therapist? That he'd never find the chance to transition? That was on the cards anyway, so big bloody deal. And it was Phyvwonoh's fault for flinging the bait.

"Are you your wife's assigned donor?" Jerome asked with a smirk on his face.

Phyvwonoh flicked his head in Jerome's direction. He stood up swiftly, sat back down in his own seat and crossed his legs.

"I'm not permitted to answer that, Mr. Beyett. You know that very well."

The clouds disappeared again. Were they a reflection of Phyvwonoh's mood?

"What if the answer to that question helped me discover what makes me happy?" Jerome said, the smirk on his face transitioning into a toothy grin.

Phyvwonoh scoffed. "I find that near impossible."

"*Near* impossible?"

Phyvwonoh clicked his tongue.

"What if the answer to that question resulted in the revelation that I wanted a career at PremsBank?" Jerome was playing with him now. He loved to tease. And this session wasn't going anywhere—as usual—so he couldn't see the harm in having a bit of fun.

Phyvwonoh sat upright and his eyes widened. "*Would* you like a career at PremsBank?"

Jerome shrugged. "Maybe. Maybe not. I wouldn't know because you didn't answer my question." He laughed and slapped his knee.

Sick and tired of Jerome's disregard for his own fate, Phyvwonoh closed his eyes and rubbed his brow. "Mr. Beyett. I urge you to take this seriously."

"I think you need to learn how to be more persuasive, Phy. I think you need therapy from *me*. I could teach you how to make jokes which could put your clients at ease."

Phyvwonoh breathed in and out, counting to four on the inhale and six on the exhale. He chanted to himself: *do not reply do not reply do not reply. Perhaps it's time to try a more radical approach. Perhaps instilling fear and guilt may be the best way to get through to this man. Yes, I was taught to not resort to threats too early in the process should the need for desperate measures arise closer to the death inducement date. But for the record, these are desperate measures. I see no sign of Jerome budging from his stubborn views and values. This is a joke to him. The whole thing. And it always will be. Unless ... there will be no more levelling with Mr. Beyett. Mr. Beyett needs a strict father figure to tell him exactly how it is and what to do. He needs to be put in his place like cattle in a cull queue. He needs to feel like a vulnerable and homeless and starving little brat who is suffering at the side of the road before tit-for-tat measures were in place—someone who finally realizes it is too late to live like a normal human being—one who would do anything for some shelter, anything to become a respected citizen of the Globe again, to make up for the people he's hurt and killed for the smallest amount of food and warmth. I've read about those desperate times, and I have no sympathy. It was all their own fault for letting themselves get into such a situation. It was the Globe's fault for allowing the health of its beings to decline. It was the establishment's fault for not being man enough to fix it. Governor Jacobson is my hero, and I am not going to let this man ruin everything he has strived for.*

So ... I am going to make him feel ...

Like a weak disposable useless peasant child.

Fear.

Guilt.

Fear.

Guilt.

Fear!

Guilt!

"Mr. Beyett," Phyvwonoh said with bite. "Your homework for tonight is to tear up your list of new career choices. You are never to consider them again. Ever. I do not even want you to think about work. In fact, the moment you leave this room, I am going to call your boss and tell him that you no longer work for him. You are now unemployed. It is no longer the life support you speak of. You will be forced to seek new employment. And if you are a success in that new position, you will receive the Letter. If you are not, you shall no longer exist.

"Once you've torn up that list, I want you to take the smallest pieces of that life you missed out on and burn them—right in front of your family. While those pieces of your possible future existence are burning, you are going to say the following:

I am a failure.

By killing myself, I have killed my father, my mother, my wife.

And by killing my wife, I am killing my daughter too.

And by killing my daughter, I am killing my grandchild.

And I don't care.

I don't care about any of you.

I am happy to watch your souls perish.

I don't love you. I hate you.

I have hated you all from the beginning.

And this is my way of finally showing you how I feel."

Phyvwonoh watched the color drain from Jerome's face. *I must not smile, no matter how much I want to. Show Jerome*

*you are serious. Because this is exactly what Jerome is doing
to his family by not caring about his own life.*

"You—can't be serious," Jerome stuttered.

"I am *very* serious," said Phyvwonoh. He walked to the
window and opened the blinds. The holographic clouds
dispersed slightly as the outdoor light flushed into the room.
He glanced down. Mrs. Beyett and little Leila sat on the
edge of the fountain by the entrance to the building.

"I can see your wife and daughter, Jerome. I suggest you
have a think about how you are going to tell them you have
just lost your job, and therefore your entire retirement fund,
which they are surely relying on to survive when you are
gone. Prepare what you are going to say right now. Because
they are outside. Waiting for you. They are laughing. They
are happy. Tell them I said I am very sorry."

WATCH

Jerome walked out of the DeathCare Centre as pale as an empty Anima urn. Selma grabbed and squeezed Leila's hand. Leila didn't squeeze back; she yanked her hand away, wrapped her arms around her belly and sat on the edge of the fountain.

Jerome approached and stood in front of them—staring right through the tumbling water at a bluebird—no hug or kiss hello, no habitual stroke of Leila's hair despite her recoiling every time he did it. The bluebird looked at Jerome but did not chirp, did not flutter by or lead him to his destination. The bluebird pecked at some stray seeds scattered along the rim of the fountain and flew away without a sound.

Suddenly the sky grew overcast and grey. Thunder cracked and lightning struck, cracking the footpath between them.

Leila screamed and launched herself into Selma's embrace. The three of them ran until they'd stepped beyond the inner circle of the building to where the Globe's natural weather was visible. As they reached the border of the weather ring, Selma held onto Jerome's upper arm and panted. "What was all that about?"

Jerome shook and turned his head. He searched the sky and quickly wiped away his tears before facing Selma. All the clouds were gone.

"That didn't have anything to do with you, did it?" Selma said with an edge of urgency in her voice.

"Probably," Leila scoffed and rolled her eyes.

Selma glared at Leila, but Jerome didn't bat an eyelid. Instead, he smiled and took their hands, his voice gentle and friendly, "Let's go check out your apartment, Leila. Let's go and do what we had planned."

Leila turned her head away from her parents' view and smiled. Selma nodded reluctantly. "I've heard strange stories about the weather ring," Selma said as they started walking to their car. "But everything seems like myth."

Jerome forced a smile that was genuine enough to fool his family.

"This afternoon is all about Leila. Let it be filled with hope, happiness, and family union. At least ... that's what Governor Jacobson would say." ...

"Leila, you must be the first to step into your new apartment." Jerome said, "That's the way it's meant to be. It's your very first step into motherhood."

Leila pursed her lips with a pause. She didn't hold her tongue. "Everything you're saying today sounds like a government campaign. Are you an idiot, or is this some kind of homework assignment from your therapist?"

Jerome bit his top lip and ran his hands along the back of the maroon velveteen sofa.

"What do you think? Great squat, isn't it?" he said.

Leila frowned, glanced at Selma and back at Jerome again with a sarcastic laugh. "It's like you're trying to show you love me without actually feeling it."

"Leila!" Selma crossed her arms, "Apologize."

Leila didn't.

Jerome manually uncrossed Selma's arms and placed them

by her sides. He whispered, "It's okay. Relax. Her behavior isn't really about me."

Selma's jaw dropped slightly in response. A muted squeal of satisfaction escaped her mouth.

Leila stood in the middle of the lounge and looked up at the ceiling. The small patch of loose paint covering a damp patch flapped as a strong gust of wind entered the room when the front door slammed shut, making everyone jump.

"Someone must have lived here before," Leila said with a look of disgust on her face. "I *hate* the thought of that." She licked her lips. "I said I wanted a *new* apartment." Leila shivered and rubbed her arms.

"It *is* new," Jerome said, with a confused pout. Leila glared.

"I'm really sorry, Sweetie." Selma added." We couldn't find a new one within our price range."

Leila glared at Jerome, who had managed to maintain his forced smile since leaving DeathCare Therapy.

"Honey," Selma said, stroking Leila's hair, "Jerome didn't know it had already been lived in. I didn't have the time to tell him."

"How could you not have had the time to tell him? It's just one fucking sentence. You see each other every day," Leila squealed. A tear ran down her cheek and hovered at the edge of her jaw.

"It didn't come up in conversation, Leila," Jerome said, sitting on a beige beanbag by the glass coffee table.

"Oh no! No!" Leila cried.

"I'm sorry. Have I missed something?" Jerome asked. "What's the big deal here?"

"You can't even do what you're meant to do!" Leila screamed. "You can't do *any*thing right. Not ever!"

Selma and Jerome looked at each other with raised eyebrows.

"Sweetie, what didn't he do right?" Selma said as gently as she could while Leila covered her face with her hands and sobbed. Jerome flicked his hand in silent question. Selma pointed to her belly with a slight shrug.

Leila sat cross-legged on the beige carpet, sobbing and heaving as if she couldn't breathe. "He was ... meant ... to take care of me. He said ... he'd take care of me. You never take care of me like. Not like you say you will!"

Jerome knelt down beside Leila on the floor and tried to hug her. Leila pushed him off. "Don't touch me. I *hate* you."

"Of course I take care you of, Leila. I work hard every day to take care of you." Jerome said.

"I hope your organs rot!" Leila spat.

Jerome stopped trying to console her. He linked his fingers together and rested his hands in his lap as the sound of Leila's sobs began to subside.

"Are you done?" Jerome said. Selma sat down on the carpet with them.

"Why didn't you get me a *new* apartment like I asked? I asked for a new one—specifically—for a reason."

"What reason, honey? Tell me," Jerome said, pressing his lips together.

"You wouldn't understand."

"Humor me," Jerome and Selma said in unison, and then gave each other a knowing smile.

"Argh!" Leila clawed her fingers and shook her hands toward the ceiling. "Fine! A girl at school told me that some souls can flee their Transition Graves to wait with loved ones who are still in the FLP. But when their loved ones transitioned, they found they were stuck in limbo forever. What if that's happened here? What if I have to spend the rest of my life knowing there is another person's soul trapped inside my walls?"

"Oh sweetie," Selma said, taking Leila's hand in hers. "It's highly unlikely that what you've heard is true. They're just campfire stories. Your friends are trying to shake you. And even if it was true, surely there is nothing wrong with these walls having housed another developing soul before you?"

Leila sniffed and looked Selma in the eye.

Selma continued, "This place is grounded in another person's past, and that's a positive thing. Their thoughts and experiences may have slipped into the cracks and soaked the walls right through with their emotions. Their *positive* emotions. Which is why we feel such a positive vibe in here. Don't you think, Jerome?"

Jerome nodded with a smile that came from the heart.

"Then why do I feel such negativity?" Leila sniffed again.

"Darling," Selma said, "don't forget that you're pregnant. Your hormones are running wild and taking your emotions with them. Trust me when I say that everything seems a lot bigger and much worse than it really is when you're pregnant. I'm speaking from experience."

Jerome laughed. "Glad I avoided that."

"No surprise there," snapped Leila.

Jerome groaned.

Selma stood and walked to the wall and leaned her head against it, letting her arms hang down in front of her. Jerome approached from behind and rubbed her back. She breathed in and out slowly and deeply for about thirty seconds before pulling herself together and leading Jerome to the sofa.

"He does the best he can, Leila," Selma said in an almost whisper. "We both do."

Leila wiped her eyes, stood up, and stormed to the front door. "I *hate* you, Dad," she said through gritted teeth. "You are nothing to me. And you will be nothing to your grandchild."

Leila stepped out of the apartment and slammed the door behind her, leaving Selma and Jerome floating in an echo.

"She knows the way home. She has keys," Selma said, rubbing Jerome's back.

Jerome laughed out of the blue.

Selma frowned in question.

"Her hormones are really giving her the guts to say exactly how she feels, aren't they?"

"That's not true, Jome."

"Of course, it is, Sma. What Globe are you living on? She's been resentful and bitter from day one, and it's never gotten any better. If anything, it's gotten worse as she grew up."

"I'm sure she didn't mean that about our grandchild. She'll come around. Especially when it's born. She'll change. She'll become a mother and everything will change."

Jerome shook his head.

They sat in silence together on the carpet, running their fingers through the soft fibers, heads down. They listened to each other breathing. To the fridge's hum. To the whoosh of cars in the street. To a backdrop of trip hop from next door.

"Jome," Selma said, lifting her head. "What happened today? What was that storm all about?"

Jerome coughed and smiled. "Nothing at all to worry about, Sma." He winked, stroking Selma's cheek and wiping away the remnants of her tears. "In fact, I think things are looking up."

"Really? Oh, Jome, that makes me so happy."

Jerome got to his feet and helped Selma up. He straightened his shirt and cleared his throat.

"Sma, I actually have to go back into the office for a while. You okay getting back home? Do you need anything?"

Selma shook her head. "What do you need to go back in for at this hour?"

Jerome scratched behind his ear and contorted his lips. "Phy has organized a private meeting with my boss." His lip twitched.

"Oh! Is he helping you out?" Selma sniffed and untangled a section of her hair at the base of her neck.

"Something like that. Yeah."

Jerome kissed Selma on the forehead, and gave her behind a little slap on his way out the door.

DEATHCARE OBSERVATION #126, NEURAL OSCILLATION REGISTRY NO. 94793475934857

Jerome stood at the corner of Haven Street and Sacrifice Avenue watching businessmen and tatters enter The Ambrosial Inn. He hadn't been in this pub for years. Mainly because he didn't drink much anymore, but also because the only company he would bump into in a place like this were his colleagues. And they were the last people he wanted to see.

But he needed a drink.

Something to help him relax.

Something to get him out of this *mess*.

As Jerome entered The Ambrosial Inn the sounds and vibrations of PredaGroove flushed through his veins, adjusting the beat of his heart to match its rhythm and helping the pace of his breathing to slide into sync. He smiled and swam through the air like a gliding fish, but his heart ached with nostalgia for a past that was not his own, and tears welled up in his eyes.

Jerome leaned on the bar and wiped the tears away with his sleeve, glancing around at the cool, collected crowd. The place was packed to the brim. People were talking. They were contented. He couldn't hear them, but their lips were moving in their wrinkle-free faces. He noticed an advert for the venue above the door: *The Ambrosial Inn—You can't run, but you can hide.* It made him feel all fuzzy inside, and he laughed out loud.

He waited for the bar stool to rise from the floor. That day they were made from an amalgamation of metal scraps from the GJ Rejection Yard.

"Cool stools, hey me sproyte?" said the barman, who sported an albino peacock feather in his French twist.

Jerome nodded and half-smiled. Sat down. Couldn't take his eyes off the barman's apricot lipstick.

"Ye look like da educated toype. Ye can read Braille, royght?" Apricot Lips asked, leaning his elbows on the bar top, and his chin on his palms. Although he *could* read Braille, Jerome didn't respond. Apricot lips was most likely going to voice what he wanted regardless. Sure enough, Jerome was right.

"Rub ye fingers under ye ass." Apricot Lips laughed. He sounded like he was choking. "Don't look so shocked, me sproyte. I mean under the base of ye bar stool."

Jerome raised his eyebrows and did as he was asked.

The stool had been signed by the artist. *Anda Volley, globe-famous sculptor and creator of PredaGroove*, it read.

"Is that what's playing?" Jerome asks.

Apricot lips frowned. He clearly didn't understand what he was referring to.

"The music. Is this PredaGroove?"

"Ah! Yes-sir-roych-ya-ah!"

Jerome nodded. Slowly. Was he supposed to order now, or should he wait until Apricot Lips asked? The last time he'd been in this pub the staff were robots that were programmed to know what you wanted to drink before you sat down. In fact, they were *his* robots. Well, the operating system was his design, at least. He wondered when they had decided to hire s again. He was glad they had. It gave the people in need a chance to earn some real cash.

"Put-cha monies on da table, me sproyte."

"Excuse me?" Jerome said, not sure he'd heard correctly.

"Show me what-chya got so I can tell ye what-chya can afford."

"Oh!" Jerome laughed. "It's okay, I can pay for my drink whatever the cost."

Apricot lips nodded and tapped his nose. "Waddle it be, den?"

"Have you got any Glenfiddich?"

Apricot Lips held an index finger to his pursed lips and feigned a thinking pose with his legs parted. The thumb of his other hand hooked into the pocket of his ripped jeans. He nodded and disappeared out back. His appearance, demeanor and voice all seemed juxtaposed from different sources, and Jerome didn't know what to make of him.

Apricot Lips returned with a bottle of Glenfiddich and slammed it on the bar top in front of Jerome. It was dusty, but genuine. He hadn't had a glass of this stuff since he was promoted at work. Quite a poignant moment, drinking it again the day he got fired. He'd come full circle. Will the circle begin again, or will GJ take a bite out of the biscuit?

"Rocks?" Apricot Lips asked.

Jerome nodded curtly.

"Real or Realthetic?"

"Realthetic." Best invention of the twenty-second century, Jerome thought. Real ice for those who don't want it to melt. Well, it does melt. Eventually. But it usually lasts for at least three refills. Also, a great way to show the bartender you intend to stay for more than one drink without letting bystanders know you can afford it. Nothing worse than a pub full of tatters bombarding you with exchange requests for a free drink.

Apricot Lips poured him a generous serving with a wink. "Looks loyke ye need it, me sproyte."

Jerome raised his glass as a thanks and took his first swig of Glenfiddich in ... he couldn't remember how long. He closed his eyes and swished it around his mouth before allowing it to slide gracefully down his throat; the velvet burn a distraction of pleasure and pain.

Bliss.

He opened his eyes as a shadow flitted across him. A young blonde lady sat next to him, dressed in a pair of loose black shorts and a red and blue flannel shirt. Her crystal nose stud, the size of a pinhead, complimented her petite figure and delicate features.

She must have been half Jerome's size. Jerome scrutinized her hand as she rested her pot of stout beer on a coaster. From the corner of his eye, he noticed blue paint under her jagged, but not bitten, fingernails. The exact same blue he'd saw inside the Anima Cemetery.

"You been working for GJ?" Jerome asked, tilting his head to the side so as not to look directly into her eyes.

She offered him a sarcastic smile and clicked her tongue with a wink. "Good old GJ."

Jerome held out his hand. "Jerome," he said.

"Bótey," said the lady, and shook his hand. "You look like a respectable bloke. What are you doin' in a place like this?"

"I used to come here back in the day. Before I—" Jerome was about to say *Before I got married*, but he slipped his wedding ring off under the bar top and slid it into his pocket instead.

"Before you ...?" Bótey puckered her brow.

Jerome laughed and scratched under his chin. "Before I became an elitist ladder climber."

"At least you're admitting to it," Bótey said, twisting around to face Jerome and raising her glass. "Cheers to that."

Jerome clinked his glass against hers with a nod. "Hope you don't mind me asking, but what do you get paid nowadays for being a GJ worker?"

"Paid? Ha!" Bótey downed the rest of her stout and gestured to Apricot Lips to bring her another. "He only hires tatters as handy workers now. For every year that I work 9 to 3, five days a week, I get three years' worth of health cover, and two ready meals per day for me and my boy."

Jerome scoffed. "Are you happy with that? Seems quite restricting to me."

Bótey nods. "It is. I still have to find time to tat for other things, like clothes, utility cover and stuff. It's not enough at all really."

Jerome frowned into his glass. "GJ's really taking the piss these days."

Bótey hooked her right foot under her thigh and jiggled her knee up and down. Jerome caught sight of her underwear. Cream-colored and decorated with bluebirds. Probably a perk that came with the job.

"So, uh ... how are you paying for those beers? If you don't mind me asking?"

Bótey grinned, bared her pearly-white teeth, and said, "blowjobs." She stood up and positioned herself between Jerome's knees, sliding her hands up his thighs.

Jerome shifted in his seat, but not enough to pull away. He looked Bótey right in the eye as she leaned in closer and licked her pink lips. His stiffening penis puckered the fly in his pants.

Apricot Lips slid Bótey a fresh pot of beer along the bar with a wink. Bótey tilted her head toward the beer and said, "That beer's on you. The head's on me."

LISTEN

The next day Jerome didn't go into work. But he did go to The Ambrosial Inn. He went to The Ambrosial Inn the day after that too, and the day after that, and the day after that, until almost an entire month had passed of pretending to go into work without Selma suspecting a thing. I know, Eve. Horrible, horrible lies.

He wasn't fulfilled. He hadn't received the Letter, and his bank account was beginning to show evidence of his non-existent employment. Phy said he was reaching the point of no return, and that he didn't "condone the frivolous activity in the slightest." But Jerome couldn't stop. He was addicted to it. He loved the way it made him feel completely numb to his fate. He could let himself go for one blissful moment, when he pulled up his fly, standing in the alleyway behind the pub on the edge of the aqueduct. He'd watch the water ebb and flow. Life was just a noun representing here and there.

But at home it didn't. There it meant something to him. Selma and Leila still had life. And he didn't want to make them miserable.

Time was running out.

It all came to a head one day when I was taking a walk with Abel to check out a new fruit shop around the corner from our squat when I saw ... it. Now before you start thinking I was betraying Selma and her bakery, I'll have you know that she is the one who suggested I go. She said that bread and sweets is not a good diet for a little boy and that the owner of the new fruit shop had recently started coming to Selma's. I didn't have to tat. She made some sort of deal with the guy as a thank you for helping her out.

But that morning I didn't make it to the new fruit shop.

As we passed the alleyway behind The Ambrosial Inn, Abel started giggling and tugged on the strap of my leather jacket.

"Mama, look!" He pointed down the alleyway at a man in a hoodie getting a blow job from an androgynous figure dressed like a peacock. Turquoise feathers extended from her head and shook—from the up and down sucking motion—like a bird experiencing a seizure. She was practically naked except for the shiny silver hot pants and bright purple stars stuck over her tiny manlike breasts. Her bare feet were filthy and calloused, like she had never worn a shoe in her life. The water was rough that day. It kept creeping up and licking the creature's heels. If she took one step backwards, she'd have fallen in.

I wanted to keep on moving, but I was mesmerized, and my feet just didn't seem to want to move. I gasped as the man ejaculated onto the woman's chest and I quickly covered Abel's eyes with my hands. The sound of my voice must have caught the man's attention because he lifted his head. He looked straight into my eyes, and though he was covered head to toe, and his hood created a shadow across his face, I knew those eyes. Those sad brown puppy dog eyes that drooped slightly at the outer edges. They sparkled as a ray of sun shifted across them just as they met mine.

They were Jerome's. *Hallelujah,* I cried in my head. I laughed out loud and quickly covered my mouth.

He recognized me and spun around, struggling to zip up his fly.

"Abel, quickly, let's go. It's just a couple having a bit of fun. Nothing to see here," I said, giving him a little nudge forward.

I had no idea how I was going to deal with this. I was so glad that our plan worked. But I certainly wasn't glad that Selma thought he wasn't going ahead with it. And I definitely wasn't glad that Abel and I had a date that night for dinner ... at Selma and Jerome's.

DEATHCARE OBSERVATION #239, NEURAL OSCILLATION REGISTRY NO. 94793475934857

"**F**uck fuck fuck," Jerome whispered between gritted teeth. He pushed Miss Peacocker off him so hard and fast that she almost fell into the water.

"Watch it, dick-for-brains. You coulda killed me," she said, straightening her feathers and adjusting her shorts.

He watched as Icasia and Abel scurried off like frightened little rabbits.

"Fuck, fuck, fuck!" he screamed into the sky, and it started to pelt down.

Someone at DeathCare was having a laugh. He knew it. He could feel it. He could feel that someone was watching his every move. Until now, he hadn't given a fuck. Because having someone you don't know spy on you is a lot better than having someone you do know, and care about, catch you cheating on your wife.

Jerome pulled his hood tight across his head and walked the deserted backstreets home to avoid bumping into a WarDen on patrol for people breaking the weekday curfew. He was always surprised by how many people were actually out and about when word on the street was that 99.5% of the population was pro GJ. He reckoned it was more like 99.5% *say* they're pro GJ out of fear, but will have no qualms about breaking the rules if they're likely to get away with it. Afterall, weekends were like out-of-uniform days. Grace periods to be yourself ... within reason.

Jerome entered a street lined with kinetic glass buildings reflecting off each other, their gills sighing as they opened and closed in response to CO2 emissions. Thumbs up for air quality, thumbs down for their spookiness, he thought, as the sun began to set and the streets eventually grew quiet.

He paused and looked at his distorted reflection in the square glass panels. He removed his hood and scrutinized the dark circles under his eyes. He hadn't slept well for days. Selma had put it down to being under stress over his impending doom. Jerome put it down to screwing everything that moved within a two-meter radius ... *and* his impending doom.

When he turned to head home once and for all, a WarDen's face appeared inches away from his own.

The WarDen stared, standing tall and stiff, his navy-blue suit as slick as a hot shot lawyer might wear, except for the silvery bluebird embroidered on his left breast pocket.

Jerome scrabbled through his own pockets for his work ID to prove he had permission to break curfew, praying the WarDen didn't scan it and discover it was no longer valid.

The WarDen squinted at the ID and then at Jerome, craning his neck.

"You're dressed rather casually for a man in your field." The WarDen's voice was deep and soft, not threatening at all, which made it even more so. The calm in his voice was like the eye of the storm.

"We, uh, had a casual dress day at the office," Jerome tried not to stammer. The consequences of breaking curfew were typically not anything more serious than a hefty fine, but if he did get fined, it would have already arrived at the house via a Jacobson representative before Jerome got home that night, and Selma would put two and two together. He wasn't ready for the consequences of destroying her trust.

"If I scan your ID, will I be disappointed in you?" the WarDen said, not moving anything at all except his mouth. Jerome's personal space was overwhelmed by spearmint breath, not to mention the fact that his feet were locked to the ground and he had no urge to resist.

"Of course not," Jerome said, mimicking the WarDen's stance.

The WarDen stepped back with a bow of his head. He said nothing else. The only way Jerome understood he was free to go was by the feeling of release around his feet and the sense that he was being praised.

Jerome had walked about five meters away from the WarDen when the sound of a cough stopped him in his tracks. He turned to see if the WarDen still stood there. He did.

"For the record, we all know," the WarDen said. "But given your situation, and your contribution to the Globe thus far, it has been decided that you are to be granted asylum."

Shit, how could I forget. Jerome thought back to the moto at the front of The Ambrosial Inn. *Bollocks.* He sniffed and rubbed a tickle from his nose. He wasn't sure if NOR was creating this sensation of unease or if it was real.

"A warning, however," the WarDen added. "should you do anything—anything at all—to put other people's lives in danger, you will be swiftly collected and culled without hesitation. Do you understand?"

Jerome stared at the WarDen's shiny black shoes. He couldn't bear to look him in the eye. He felt like he was ten years old again and his father had caught him playing by the Aqueduct when he was told not to. Disappointing his father brought on the greatest shame. Jerome constricted his throat to stop the tears.

"I understand," Jerome said with a slight nod, still looking at the WarDen's feet.

"Be well," the WarDen said, and vanished into thin air.

WATCH

Selma set the table in silence while Jerome stirred through the pot of sticky salmon risotto, humming the abstract tune from The Ambrosial Inn.

"That new PredaGrove style is interesting isn't it?" Selma pulled out a chair and sat down, flattening the tablecloth with her hands without disturbing the perfectly aligned cutlery with subtle bluebirds etched into the handles.

Jerome paused, wooden spoon mid stir, and glared into the pot.

"Yeah. It's got something. What were you doing at The Ambrosial Inn?" he asked.

Selma's nostrils flared. She banged her hand on the table, managing to disturb some of the cutlery this time. Jerome jumped and turned around.

"What's got into you, Sma?" Jerome's Adam's apple bobbed as he swallowed. The silence in the room was so thick that you could hear saliva navigating their mouths and throats.

"Don't try to pull the wool over my eyes by turning this on me. What do you take me for? Do you really think I'm that stupid?"

Jerome shrugged.

"The bank called today," Selma whispered through gritted teeth.

Jerome sighed with slight relief.

"Sma, I can explain—"

The doorbell rang.

Selma pulled her Comm out of her pocket and texted Icasia: *the door is open.*

A few seconds later Icasia and Abel were standing in the arched entrance of the kitchen, smiling. Icasia glanced at Jerome and blushed. He shook his head.

Icasia readjusted her smile and squeezed Abel's shoulders. "Sorry it's taken so long to introduce you to my son. Jerome, Selma, meet Abel. Abel, these are the generous people I've been telling you about."

Abel stepped toward Selma and held out his hand. "Pleased to meet you, Miss Selma."

Selma grinned from ear to ear. She took Abel's hand to shake it, but Abel bowed and kissed her hand instead.

Everyone laughed.

"You're quite the gentleman, aren't you?" Selma said, patting the chair next to hers. "Come. Take a seat. I hope you like rice and salmon?"

"Yes, I doooo," Abel said, moving his head up and down, unable to take his eyes off Jerome.

Icasia whispered, "He's never had it before," and sat on the opposite side of the table. She gently kicked Abel's leg under the table and mouthed, "Stop staring."

Abel screwed up his mouth and glanced at Jerome one more time before blurting out, "Are you the man that was naked with the peacock?"

Icasia laughed like the canned laughter they once used in sitcoms.

"No silly!" Icasia said a little aggressively as she watched Jerome's face grow red. "That was just some random drunk."

"But he's wearing the same clothes," Abel mumbled. A

small tear escaped and rolled down his cheek. He wiped it on his shoulder.

Jerome faced the stove and stirred the risotto, clenching the wooden spoon until his knuckles whitened.

Selma stood and approached Jerome's side. She placed her hand over his that held the wooden spoon.

"The risotto is ready, Jerome. I'll serve it now." Their eyes met. Jerome's glazed over as if he were about to cry. Selma held his stare until he turned away.

Jerome released the wooden spoon and smiled at Icasia and Abel before leaving the room without a word.

Selma took each plate from the table and filled it with risotto, scooping up the slush from the pot, hitting the bottom of the plates a little too hard with the spoon. Abel kicked the leg of the table. Over and over and over again.

Selma slopped risotto into Jerome's plate so hard that it splattered all over the table. She hurled the wooden spoon across the room and broke down in tears. Abel gasped and sobbed. Icasia squeezed his hand in consolation and went round to his side of the table to hug him around the shoulders.

"Why didn't you tell me?" Selma heaved and spluttered between words.

"I'm sorry. I thought it better to wait 'til tomorrow." Icasia squeezed Abel's hand again and whispered, "It's okay. It's not your fault." She stood up and reached out to embrace Selma. Selma didn't move, but allowed Icasia to wrap her arms around her, squeezing her elbows into her torso. Selma's body shook in silence, interrupted only when gasping for air.

"Mama, I want to go home," Abel said.

"I'm sorry. We should go. Tonight was a bad idea," Icasia half-whispered.

Selma nodded with jagged breaths and wiped her eyes with her forearms.

"See you tomorrow?"

Selma nodded again and walked Icasia and Abel to the door.

As she opened the front door and ushered them out, she spotted a bluebird hovering above a little nest, tucked behind the porch light.

"Am I doing this all wrong?" she whispered to the bluebird. "Are the four letters in *life* representing the wrong word?"

DEATHCARE OBSERVATION #242, NEURAL OSCILLATION REGISTRY NO. 94793475934857

Jerome sobbed on the bathroom floor with his head between his knees. Selma leaned into the door frame with her arms crossed and looked at her feet.

"I'm not angry, Jerome," she said, letting her arms hang loosely by her sides. She slid her body down the doorframe into a cross-legged position on the floor; one knee inside the bathroom, the other in the hall. Jerome lifted his head and glared at Selma, tears streaming down his cheeks. When he first came into the bathroom, he'd cried too hard and too fast. His head pounded and snot blocked his nose. Selma got to her feet again, cleared her throat, and dragged the footstool over from the sink to sit on.

"I know you did exactly what I wanted you to do, Jerome," Selma said with conviction. "But I'm not going to pretend that this hasn't come as a surprise, and I'm not going to deny that I am extremely hurt—more by your lies than your unfaithfulness."

Jerome sniffed. Selma was right. Lying was the worst thing anyone could inflict on a marriage. So many times he'd wanted to confess. So many times he'd said to himself, *today you tell her.* So many times, he'd—

"I've always thought of you and me as a team," Selma interrupted when he opened his mouth to apologize. "But this is not teamwork, Jerome. This is a one-sided struggle for survival. And I feel like *I'm* the one doing the struggling, and you're just giving up. And it's not just your survival, Jerome. It's my survival too, and Leila's, and your parents'. This isn't about trying to save a life. This is about trying to save a family."

Jerome nodded, head tucked between his knees, staring at his feet. A tear dropped from his nose onto the light blue tiled floor. Selma dragged herself closer to Jerome and rested her hand on his forearm. He trembled, and she squeezed his arm. She smiled a little and lowered the volume of her voice.

"You know how puzzle pieces get lost if there is no box? Well, this family is the box, Jome. And without this family, we will all be lost. You are a piece of the bigger picture, and the picture belongs to all of us. So, I need you to do something for me, Jome. I need you to stop being selfish—*I* need to stop being selfish too, because this isn't just about you and me. I need you to look at this like you are saving your family from a terrible car crash. The car is upside down, Jome, and the fuel tank is about to blow up. I'm betting you'd do your best to pull your family out of that car wreck, right?"

Selma slipped off the footstool and knelt on the floor. She cupped Jerome's face in her hands and kissed his trembling bottom lip.

"Do not let us go up in flames, Jome."

"I—I won't." Jerome stammered and shook his head like a little boy.

Selma hung her head. "How?"

"By finding happiness?"

"And to find happiness we need to find out what is making you so miserable, and reverse it. So, talk to me,

Jome. Tell me—" Selma spread her fingers over Jerome's chest, "what's in here? Tell me what is really *in* here."

Jerome shrugged and started to sob again. Selma pushed herself backwards and leaned her head against the wall.

Jerome lay on the floor and stared at the ceiling. He didn't blink for so long that for a moment, Selma thought he'd lost consciousness. But he was just lost in his thoughts. How had he turned into such a misplaced and helpless little boy? Where did the man go that Selma first met? Where did his ambition go? He used to talk about all the wild and wonderful things he was going to invent, how he was going to change the way people thought about robots, how he would make people stop seeing them as a threat and embrace their existence, their beauty, their potential to serve society and make the Globe a better place. He became discouraged when a younger and apparently more innovative colleague scored the promotion he'd been working for all his life. He soon lost his drive to create, and work became just a job that put food on the table.

Jerome closed his eyes and tried to meditate. He noticed the way his hair had flopped onto the pale blue tiles like a sea of black matted fur. He was aware of his wet eyelashes, his jagged nails, and the stubble on his face. He had let himself go. If he didn't start talking about his feelings soon, all hope would be lost. Phyvwonoh was useless. Forcing him out of his job had just made things worse. But he still didn't believe that finding a new job would make things any better. There was only one thing he knew he was right about—that there wasn't enough time to find motivation from a new career. It had to be something else; there had to be some sort of loophole. Something that would arrive unannounced out of the left field and surprise him and everybody else.

Maybe it was a combination of things no one was aware

of—even the experts at the Neural Oscillation Registry. Or maybe it wasn't even 'things' at all. Maybe it was just an indescribable feeling. Jerome remembered the times by the aqueduct, the single malts in the Ambrosia Inn, the days when he'd felt there was nothing in the entire Globe that could possibly make him feel that positivity, that sense of expectation and heady optimism he'd once had. Even if that feeling didn't last, he'd at least got to feel it, if only ephemerally. Maybe it was relief. Maybe it was freedom from his own agitated, powerless and vulnerable thoughts. Jerome had never been sure what shape or form happiness came in, but he was sure it could exist for everyone in some shape or form.

He reminded himself about the advice he'd offer to his weary colleagues: *It's never too late for anything.*

"Why ..." Selma paused, "Why haven't you been to visit Leila since she moved out?" Selma pinched the bridge of her nose.

Jerome had stopped crying. He had closed his eyes and laced his fingers across his ribcage, and his hands rose and fell steadily as he breathed.

"She doesn't need me," he whispered. "She needs you."

"That's not true. She needs both of us."

"Sma—" Jerome shook his head side to side and tsked. "She doesn't love me."

Selma puckered her brow. "But ... why does that matter? You are her father. She doesn't need to love you. *You* need to love *her*."

"Leila has hated me ever since the day I set foot into this house."

"Jome—"

"No. No matter what I do to show her I love her, it makes no difference. Leila and I are not solvable."

"But ..." Selma's breath caught in her throat. "*Do* you? Do you love her?"

Jerome turned his head and looked Selma in the eye. He felt something he hadn't felt before. Remorse, shame and guilt—all rolled into one.

"Sma, I—" Jerome frowned and swallowed as though he had a sore throat. "I'm not really sure if I ever have."

LISTEN

The morning after that dinner—or I guess that absence of dinner, since we hadn't stayed to eat—the door chimed as I entered the bakery like the soundtrack to a revelation. But I tamed the thought until I'd had the chance to gauge Selma's emotional state. The past couple of months had consisted of little more than anxious conversations that led nowhere except the kitchen to help Selma bake. It seemed to be the only thing that kept her mental state in check.

But that morning was different, Eve. Not only was Selma's face tear free, but she had a whole different aura about her. She handed me my morning coffee and a plum pastry with an expression of determination, and gestured toward the table and chairs with her chin.

"Sit," she said. "We have to talk."

For a moment I thought I was in trouble for something, until we sat down and she gently placed her hand on top of mine, slipping her index finger just below the cuff of my leather jacket.

I puckered my brow and said, "Are you—?" I was going to ask if she was okay, but she interrupted.

"Jerome told me something very interesting last night."

I thought she was referring to the blowjob in the alleyway. I blurted out a mess of apologies for not letting her know and lame reconciliations for his behavior.

"Icasia—" Selma held two fingers to my lips and shook her head. "Shh." The right side of Selma's mouth turned upward. "He said he thinks Leila doesn't love him, and he's not sure if he has ever loved her either."

I craned my neck inward. "Selma, that's *it*. I was going to suggest this morning that all we want to feel is needed—appreciated—indispensable. That's why most people receive the Letter after they get promoted, or receive an award at work or feel satisfied with their career. Because for those people work was their life, and because it was their life it was the thing that gave them the greatest emotional stability. They knew they were indispensable, and finally felt safe and appreciated. Maybe that's why Jerome has never received the Letter and you have."

Selma shook her head and took a sip of coffee.

"Wait, hear me out," I said. "When I walked into the bakery that first morning, I needed you to feed me and Abel. In most cases this feeling of being needed happens in the work-place because even though we are technically needed by our family members, it's not a constant for us. Being needed by family fluctuates, depending on mood. And this kind of uncertain dependency doesn't satisfy that deeper desire to be fully recognized for everything we do. Make sense?"

Selma nodded, a little uncertain. "Go on."

I was feeling proud of myself in that moment, I must say, Eve. I sounded like a true writer. A philosopher even.

"Well, it's clear to me now," I continued, "that Jerome's situation is different. He lost faith in his job long ago. The only thing left is his family, and it seems that no one in his family needs him anymore. Leila's been inseminated and you have me and the bakery. It's clear to Jerome that if his soul were to be annihilated, that you and Leila would do just fine without him. He's not a necessity in anyone's life but his own.

"That can't be it," Selma said. "I tell him so many times that I need him here. That I can't live without him, that there's no way I can imagine moving into my Transition Grave without knowing we will meet on the other side."

"But they're just words," I said. "Don't you see that it doesn't matter what anyone says unless that person can actually feel it in their heart?"

Selma shrugged. She wasn't convinced. So, I pulled out my Comm and accessed the library. I searched for *How does the Neural Oscillation Registry work*, and pulled up a Jacobian article entitled, *The Secret of the Letter*. I read it out to her:

Neural oscillation levels are observed and recorded at the Central Circuit Hub of the Neural Oscillation Registry via an electrode that is embedded just after birth above the oscillatory gland under the scalp. After decades of research, it has been concluded that certain frequencies of oscillation are linked to the perception and awareness of success and a deeply rooted subconscious sense of satisfaction and content- ment that results from that success. It has also been widely documented that citizens who experience this sense of what we like to refer to as 'happiness' are less likely to question the meaning of life, which in turn leads to calm, rational, law-abiding citizens who are 98.7% less likely to disrupt the peace. The Jacobson Movement therefore promotes a way of life which is likely to guide people toward experiencing this subconscious state of mind. Citizens whose neural oscillations register in the gamma frequency band for more than three hours at a time will receive the Letter, which gives them permission to move into the Second Life Phase as they have reached a state of mind which will prevent them from hurting themselves or others, intentionally or otherwise, due to a lack of self-worth.

Selma stared at her fingers, which were clasped around her mug.

"So ... you think they're wrong about this?" she said, slightly confused.

"No, I'm saying that this is just research, and it says that their suggested way of living is *likely* to lead to this state of mind. *Likely* does not mean *definitely*, right?"

Selma shook her head in what seemed like agreement, leaned back in her chair and crossed her arms. "But it doesn't make sense," she said. "Why do all the advertisements promote how to become successful if they don't know for sure?"

"Once upon a time people didn't fully trust what the media said. I read that the government used the media to persuade people to think things that would benefit their own selfish needs and fill their own bank accounts."

"I don't think that's what is happening here," Selma said, crossing her legs.

"Neither do I," I said. "But I do think that the media was created to make everybody feel like there are solutions to problems no one really knows the answers to. Imagine what the world would be like if everyone felt uncared for, okay? It makes people accept how things are, not ask questions and just get on with their lives. But I think we *need* to ask questions if we are going to figure this out. I think there is way more to our oscillation frequencies than the documented literature lets on. I mean, it doesn't make sense for them to be 100% sure. Scientists will never know everything there is to know about the brain."

Just as Selma was about to agree, a semi-overweight, freckled man with a ginger beard walked in and custom ordered a cake.

"What's the occasion?" Selma asked.

"I just got me friggin' letter this mornin'!" He squealed like a girl and jumped from one leg to the other, fist-pumping the air.

I spun around in my chair, eager to ask the guy why he got it, but Selma beat me to it.

"Congratulations, Sir. If you don't mind me asking, what did you do to deserve it?"

He stopped still and looked at her with and expression of disbelief. "Deserve it? How do you mean?"

"What happened in your life for you to receive the Letter?" Selma said.

The customer frowned and stroked his beard.

"You know what? I dunno," he said. "Nothing out-of-the-ordinary happened at me job now I come to think 'bout it. Maybe 'cause I just been there for freakin' ever. Proved meself, y'know?"

Selma raised her eyebrows and glanced at me. I opened my mouth to speak, and she nodded in my direction. I got out of my seat and introduced myself to the guy, reacquainting myself with my aspiring writer's role.

"Do you mind if I ask you a couple of questions? For research?"

"Aw, I dunno. I really should be gettin' back." He put his hands in his pockets and rolled backwards and forwards on the balls of his feet a couple of times.

"It'll only take a minute," I said. I spotted Selma gesturing with her hands and silent lips for me to offer him a free coffee.

"Would you like coffee and cake on the house?" I said.

The man's face lit up. "Yeah, awright. Go on then," he said.

We sat at the table with an extra plum pastry while Selma went out back and made his coffee. I pulled a notebook out of my bag—I had to keep up appearances—and started asking questions.

"Think back to yesterday. What did you do? Not just at work, but at home, and in between tasks. I want to know everything, even down to the smallest detail."

The man nodded, and took a bite of his pastry that left flakes in his beard. He rested his right ankle on his left knee, picking away at something stuck to the bottom of his army boot as he chewed and swallowed.

"Well, I went to work as usual. Got me coffee and toast in the worker's tent. I'm a construction supervisor, but a paid one. None of that tat malarky."

I had to hold my tongue, Eve. It was hard, but I did it.

"I rounded up me team. Told 'em the day's jobs, and assigned me individual team members a few things to be lookin' out for. Usually there are some problems that come up, so it's betta to know what they could be before they 'appen."

I nodded in interest, but felt like this wasn't going to get us anywhere.

"Nothin' 'appened that wasn't what usually 'appens. Then I went home."

"What happened when you went home?"

The man shrugged. "I ate me tea. I had a beer. Me and the wife, er ... well, you get me drift."

I sucked in a big breath through clenched teeth. This man was a pure wordsmith. I didn't know how to contain myself... Glad I could make you laugh, Eve.

"Look," I said, as Selma placed the guy's coffee in front of him with a smile. She glanced at me with hope. Begging me to continue. I knew there had to be something that happened during this guy's typical day that he didn't think was significant but probably was. "Think back again. Did anything happen, anything at all, no matter how insignificant it seems, that was a one-off, or something that made you feel good about yourself?"

"I always feel good about meself." The man laughed. His belly wobbled and shook the table a little. "But nah, yeah, look, I dunno really. Me life is simple. I like simple."

A little fire kindled in my chest at the sound of the words 'happy' and 'simple.' There must be some kind of link, I thought.

"Is that something you've known all your life, or is it something you've just started feeling recently?"

The guy shrugged again. It was getting tiresome. I felt like telling him there were other ways of expressing doubt.

"Me whole life, I guess." he said. "I've never been the go-getter type. Me wife and me were kinda startin' to accept that we wouldn't be getting any letter. But she got one this morning too. Is that fate or what?" He chuckled.

"Your wife got one too?" I was getting excited. I felt tingles go down my arms and I started scribbling all this down in my notebook. "Do you know why your wife got the Letter?"

"Yeah, absolutely. No problem there. She scored a job at PremsBank." My heart sank. It was common knowledge that all those who worked in the public sector received a free pass into the Second Life Phase. It was something to do with a different frequency of neural oscillation that allowed this. Something to do with learning dedication and obedience. Their spouses were also granted a free pass. I was never too certain of the logic in that, but I guess they couldn't be supporting family union and then go tearing apart the families of those who dedicated their lives to the cause. This guy was clearly dumber than I'd anticipated.

I smiled politely and snapped my notebook shut. "Thank you for your time. Enjoy your coffee."

I went out back to tell Selma what had happened, but she'd heard the whole thing. She'd been sitting on the floor behind the front counter. She crawled across the floor into the back room and pulled me into an embrace.

"Thank you," she said.

"What for? That whole conversation was useless."

"No, thank you for being here. I couldn't survive this without you."

Selma cupped my cheek in her hand, and I closed my eyes. I gave in to the weight of my head and leaned into her hand. I covered her hand in mine and kissed her inner wrist. She smelled of sweet tangerine. For a moment I lost sight of myself, and who I was with. The affection seemed so natural, instinctual—right.

Selma moved her hand away and I opened my eyes, afraid that I would see an expression of horror on her face—or at the very least, embarrassment. But that wasn't the case at all.

We kissed.

I had always cringed at the cliché that falling in love felt like floating on clouds. But I honestly can't think of any other way to describe what that kiss did to me. I had known for a long time that I wasn't interested in men, but I just thought it was because I wasn't interested in transitioning. The idea that I might be interested in the same sex had never occurred to me.

I gently pulled away and rested my fingers on my lips. I blushed. Selma smiled a knowing smile and pushed a strand of hair behind my ear.

"We can't even begin to consider this," she said.

Eve, my jaw dropped. She was the one who'd instigated it.

"Not until I know that Jerome is safe."

I took a deep breath and nodded. I leaned my head against the wall behind me and looked at the ceiling, puffing up my cheeks on the exhale.

I didn't know what was going on in my heart at that moment, but something inside me changed. I was no longer doing this for myself or for Abel. I was doing this because it felt right. I was doing this for the greater good. And I knew, right then and there, that Selma's kiss could have made me even more selfish. It could have motivated me to get Jerome to psychosomatic safety so that I could pursue a love affair with Selma. But it didn't. Suddenly I was able to see through the eyes of all those people like Selma. Like Jerome and Leila. Like me. All those people who suffered, who conformed to the system as little as possible in order to hold onto some dignity, but who also needed to be taken care of because the system was so much bigger than they could ever fathom. It was a fine line we straddled, and it was no easy way to live. We could have taken the easy way. Just done everything by the Book. But we felt bigger than that. We felt we could rewrite the Book. Even though we might never find the courage to do so, the possibility maintained our sense of self-respect.

I decided, then and there, that no matter what happened between Selma and me, that even if I failed with Jerome, I would continue the search for the real truth behind the Letters. I was convinced there was so much more to learn. And I was going to learn it. I was going to document it, and inspire people with it.

I was going to become *someone*.

DEATHCARE OBSERVATION #384, NEURAL OSCILLATION REGISTRY NO. 94793475934857

J erome sat in silence, watching his father, Gary, leaning forward in the armchair Jerome usually occupied. With his elbows rested on his knees, rubbing his hands together as if applying moisturizer, Gary winked in Selma's direction as a cue for her to get on her way.

"Are you sure I can't get you anything else before I head over to Leila's, Gary?" Selma asked. She wore an apricot-colored frock—a huge detour from her usual slick black attire. Jerome noticed that it accented her orange hair nicely. She'd told Jerome before Gary arrived that she hoped it would brighten the mood in the house, but she fully intended to change before she left. "If anyone in public sees me like this," she'd said, "they'd think I'd gone loopy."

Selma straightened her skirt and stood in front of Jerome and Gary, half-paralyzed. "Okay, I'll be off then," she said. She stared awkwardly, and they stared back. Jerome clicked his tongue in his cheek and Gary raised his eyebrows in question.

Selma nodded and followed the motions of an uncharacteristic half-curtsey, half-bow.

Jerome squinted and silently chuckled. *It's the dress,* he thought. *She doesn't feel herself in it.*

"Okay, I'm *going* going *gone,*" she said, and walked out with a swish.

Gary leaned toward the coffee table and scooped up a handful of peanuts using all four fingers of his right hand. He cracked the peanuts out of their shells, one by one, as he talked, resting the shells on his left thigh.

"You invited me here to talk, son," Gary said while chewing. "What is it you need to say?"

"Dad," Jerome said, rubbing his hands over his face, "it makes it really difficult for me to talk when you're so demanding. You scrutinize everything that comes out of my mouth."

Gary sniffed as if he'd breathed in an insect. He stopped cracking nuts, rubbed the crumbs off his hands onto a napkin and sat next to Jerome on the couch. Gary's body heat suffused Jerome's entire left side. It made Jerome feel uneasy, yet strangely comforted.

"Son, I know this is a very difficult time for you. Every time I think about never seeing your mother again it sets me on a rollercoaster of tears until I fall asleep. I know you think I'm a cold-hearted emotionless man, but—"

Jerome scoffed and shook his head.

"Son, you could at least do me the courtesy of letting me finish what I'm saying."

Jerome looked Gary in the eye, feeling the same shame he had always felt when his father told him off. Somehow, he always made having respect seem like having no feelings at all.

"Look," Gary said, resting a hesitant hand on Jerome's upper back. It caught Jerome by surprise. They didn't touch. They had never even hugged. "What I'm trying to say, son, is that I can understand a little about your feelings."

Jerome scoffed again. He couldn't help himself. He thought the hand on his back might have meant he was softening up. "Do you really understand though, Dad?" he said. "This grief you're feeling for Mum is just between you and her. If I don't make it, Dad, it's like Selma says. I'm setting my whole family on fire. You're all relying on me to live and I can't take the responsibility and the pressure, Dad. I honestly can't take it anymore. I—, I—"

Despite summoning all his will power to not succumb to Gary's presence, Jerome fell into his father's stiff embrace and cried into his shoulder. He never used to let himself do this. He hated showing his emotions. It made him feel weak. It made him feel like Leila couldn't rely on him for support. It was too late now anyway. The days of him being the strong reliable father were over. He scolded himself for buckling at his father's touch.

Gary still didn't loosen up. Jerome's quick heartbeat pumped on Gary's arm when he hugged him so tightly that it caused a little crack to escape from Gary's throat. He wondered why he had never hugged his father in all these years and realized, at that very moment, that he hadn't always acted so cold.

They'd pretend to be on archaeological missions and imaginary mountain hikes in their backyard, and when Jerome found some scrap metal that resembled miniature robots one day, Gary had praised his mock-commentary, hugged him, and told him he was proud to be his father; that one day he would become everything he ever wanted in a son. When did that stop? Why did bad memories always cloud the good ones? Why hadn't he ever had any moments like this with Leila? The heavy pull of regret in his stomach made him feel ill.

Gary guided Jerome into a sitting position again and held

him upright by his shoulders. "I've been hard on you, son. I know, and for that I'm sorry. I am truly sorry. But I thought that if I was tough on you that you'd grow a tough skin yourself. I was wrong about that. We are different people, and I never took the time to consider that my actions might be doing more harm than good. I've done too much talking and not enough listening over the years. For this, I am also sorry. But son, please know that whatever happens, I will always love you. I will never blame you if I am unable to see your mother again. I promise you that. The last thing I ever wanted was for my son to feel like his parents were a burden."

Jerome pushed his hair out of his eyes and glanced at the opposite side of the room where all their family photographs stood on the mantel above the FotoFire.

"But we *are* a burden as parents, Dad." Jerome sniffed. "Whether we want to be or not. In all Governor Jacobson's glory and his attempts to keep families united, he is splitting them up and breaking people's hearts. Why did you always vote for his new bills, Dad? Why did you believe in this hollow establishment? I never understood that." Jerome shook his head and repeated in a whisper, "I never understood."

The light dimmed in Jerome's eyes, and flickered, as if just barely managing to stay alive. They sat in silence for a moment while Jerome collected his thoughts and his courage. He'd wondered if he should tell Gary about his affairs—but that could cause an extra unwanted rift between them. Withholding it wouldn't do any good either. He never wanted to be a dishonest man. He just wanted to be a man, a husband, a father—a person who sparked change. He didn't need the recognition, only the result. But he couldn't even achieve that.

"There something you need to know, son." Gary rubbed his hands up and down his thighs and then stood up. He paced in front of the mantel with his hands in his pockets, his gaze locked onto some object in the distance that neither of them could see. Why couldn't he look Jerome in the eye?

"Your mother and I were one of the last influential radicals still protesting about the change. We were bribed by Governor Jacobson to get off the street. Our popularity was a threat to his Transition Grave Bill, because back then people still listened when people challenged the government with reasonable questions. We had reasonable questions. And we voiced them. But then... you got cancer."

"I—I what?" Jerome stopped slouching and sat up straight.

Gary still didn't make eye contact. He paced back and forth in front of the mantel, still focusing on the same invisible object. "We almost lost you, son. You were very, *very* young, too young to remember. We were advised to never tell you because it might affect your ability to prepare for the future. They thought that if you knew life was so fallible, you wouldn't spend time building a safety net. They were doctors. We still trusted doctors. We listened, son. We wanted you to live a long life."

"I can't believe this. You're saying that—"

"I'm saying that you're damn lucky to be alive, Jerome. You have fight in you. You had a 0.2% chance of survival and you came through. If there's anything you know how to do, son, it's how to stay alive."

"Dad, I'm confused. What has this got to do with you supporting the establishment?"

Gary hesitated, clearing his throat. His hands trembled and he slid them into his pockets. Jerome understood he was trying to hide his vulnerability. He was brought up thinking that a father should be strong for his child. That he should show his children how to be gallant and courageous, not how to crumble under pressure. Suddenly those notions were becoming less concrete.

"They offered us a deal," Gary said, squinting at his target and picking up his pace again. "If we vowed, in a court of law, to keep our mouths shut about our objections and the potential failings of the Transition Graves, he'd pay us out. The Sats were enough to last three lifetimes, son. So, we took it. I said it was an inheritance. I supposed in some odd sense it was. But it saved you. And I don't regret the choice I made. But it's funny, really, that the things we said about the potential pitfalls have now come true. Transition graves are filling up. And people are being forced to die prematurely, their souls destined to evaporate into thin air. I knew it would happen. *We* knew it would happen. Just maybe not so soon."

"So, you've been lying to me my whole life?" Jerome said, the pitch in his voice rising slightly. "Is that supposed to make me feel better? What exactly do you think this is going to achieve now?"

Gary's cheeks and nose grew red. "I—I was hoping, son, that you'd understand that people can come back from a nightmare and still have a life worth living."

"You think this life is worth living?" Jerome shouted and kicked the table. The bowl of peanuts shook to the edge and almost tipped off. "Living in constant fear of disappointing everyone who is relying on you? Tell me Dad, what is it about *this* that's worth living?" Jerome gestured to the air, to the Globe, to the little insignificant existence that surrounded him.

Gary stopped pacing. They both glanced toward shadows of movement behind the closed loungeroom door. Jerome walked up to it and rested his ear on its surface. He heard

Selma breathing and typing on her Comm. He was relieved she hadn't left.

"Love," Gary said, regaining Jerome's attention. "Life is worth living for love, son."

"Love?" Jerome said with a smirk that embodied self-loathing. "I'm not sure if I know what love feels like anymore."

Gary nodded, looked at his feet and pulled his hands out of his pockets. He stepped closer to Jerome and grabbed him by both shoulders. They finally made eye contact. Tears welled up in both men's eyes.

"I believe," Gary said, glancing at his Jerome's chest, "that's the root of your problem, son."

LISTEN

After Gary's visit, Selma was convinced that fixing the relationship between Jerome and Leila could be a solution. So the next day we asked them to come together and talk through their issues.

Perhaps it *was* love that would save Jerome. And if anything, it could shed some light on Jerome's state of mind that could at least lead to Jerome accomplishing something that would grant him the Letter. Gary said he had always been a strong believer in the power of the mind, and that the first step to a healthy mind was self-belief. And this, he said, was something Jerome definitely didn't have.

He was a wise man, Eve.

But I wasn't entirely convinced that all he needed was love to receive the Letter. One, Selma loved him. And after all these years, I couldn't understand how Jerome wouldn't love her back. Surely he did. It was obvious in his behavior. If he didn't love her, then I couldn't see any reason why he would be so broken up about hurting her. And two, I had fallen for Selma. I loved my parents, and I loved my son. I loved her. And I hadn't received the Letter.

I humored them. In spite of everything, I still believed it had something to do with feeling needed and safe. This intervention might possibly have led to releasing that emotion too, so I went along with it. Jerome's own daughter, regardless of their lack of any blood relationship, didn't need him. And that would no doubt be crushing to a father's self-worth.

I helped Selma facilitate this intervention by telling Leila that my son needed a friend to play with. Leila jumped at the opportunity to 'practice being a mother,' which made me feel even more guilty for lying. I left Abel with my parents. I didn't want him to feel uncomfortable about what had happened at dinner that night. I had every intention of bringing him again, but I needed to give it some more time.

"What's going on?" Leila shrieked when she entered the living room and saw Jerome sitting on the couch between me and her mother. "I thought I was coming to play with Abel?" Leila glared at me like she was concocting an evil spell.

"I lied," I said. I didn't think there was any point in trying to conceal anything. I thought I might try to save whatever relationship I had with Leila, as flimsy at it might have been, later. Because at that point in time, it was someone else's turn.

"I'm leaving," she snapped and spun around on one foot. Selma called out, "No! Hear us out. Please." Before Selma had even finished her plea, Leila slammed the front door behind her.

I ran after her and blocked her way in the middle of the front lawn.

"If you leave," I said, panting a little, "your child will not have any grandparents. Is that what you really want? To bring your child up in isolation with only you to turn to?"

Leila screwed up her mouth and crossed her arms over her belly. Her child kicked hard enough to make her wince. "It will have a grandmother, and that's all I care about."

"I wouldn't be so sure about that, Leila."

"What do you mean?" Leila's eyes glowed with resentment.

"I mean," I said, pulling down on the corners of my jacket to collect myself while concocting a logical reason on the spot, "it's common nowadays for partners to opt for having their souls annihilated together in the hope that they will remain joined for eternity." I had no choice but to get creative.

"What?" Leila screeched. "Did Mum say that she was going to do that?"

I remained silent for a moment, keeping eye contact with Leila to be sure she didn't sense that I was bluffing.

"Come back inside. Do this for your mother." I rested my hands gently on Leila's pulsing belly. "And her."

Leila calmed and smiled. I knew the only way into Leila's mind was through her unborn child. To Leila it was an escape from the reality at home she disliked so much. It gave her purpose and a sense of control. She would finally be a respected adult instead of a conditional child. Even though my parents had never left my side, I knew the feeling well. Not that long ago I'd been in the exact same situation. And despite the fact that having a child made me grow up fast, it wasn't fast enough. The biggest lesson I learned was that you never really grow up, and you never really know anything ... until you do. And when you do, the clarity is deafening.

"How did you know?" Leila half-whispered.

I shrugged. Lucky guess, Eve.

I walked Leila back inside. Selma clasped her hands together in relief.

Despite having gone over and over what we were going to say and how I was going to get the ball rolling, I clammed up.

Eve, it was very embarrassing. The three of them sat there on the couch. Selma looked at me with hopeful squinty eyes, Jerome looked at me with droopy depressed eyes, and Leila's eyes were closed. It looked as though she was trying to coerce herself into being okay with this.

Selma puckered her brow and raised her shoulders. I had to start speaking otherwise I'd have risked Leila leaving again, but I'd forgotten what I was supposed to say. Instead, I blurted out, "I'm love with your mother, Leila."

Don't laugh, Eve. I know. I felt crazy.

Selma gasped and covered her mouth with her hand. Leila said, "What the fuck?" And Jerome pissed himself laughing.

"I'm kidding," I said. I wasn't. I smiled sheepishly. "But now that Leila knows what it might feel like to have two mothers, maybe she can feel better about having one mother and one father. Leila, can you please tell us exactly what it is about your father that you dislike so much?"

I know, I know. I had to save myself somehow. And I know it sounded fake, but how else was I supposed to continue, to get the conversation back on track?

Leila's angry expression returned. She hugged her belly and squeezed her eyes shut. Silence.

"Leila, honey," Selma whispered. "Please answer honestly. I can't be without your father. This is going to help him. Please?"

Leila opened her eyes and gave a curt nod. I was honestly shocked. I wasn't expecting Leila to give in, considering she was such a stubborn young lady.

"I don't like the way he talks to me," she said. "Like I've always done something wrong and I'm an idiot. Like my feelings are something that I should be scolded for. I can't help feeling down sometimes. But wanting to be alone doesn't mean I'm stupid."

"I don't think you're stupid, and I don't think you're always doing something wrong, Leila," Jerome said, sitting forward on the couch, trying to make eye contact with her. But she didn't look at him. She stared at me, constantly, as if trying to make me disappear with her thoughts.

"It's just when you snap at me all the time, it becomes personal," Jerome said. I silently congratulated him for cushioning his statement with a similar tone to how a teenager would express himself. But it didn't take long for him to sound like himself again. "While I understand you're going through a very big change in your life right now, it doesn't explain why you have treated me with the utmost disrespect from the very first day I moved in here. Even as a young girl you detested me. I'm really sorry, but I very much doubt you can blame that on your current state of mind."

Leila sniffed and whipped her head in Jerome's direction. "You're doing it now, can't you see? You're speaking to me like I'm a complete idiot. Listen to that tone. Can't you hear it Mum? It's totally fucking patronizing. It's like he thinks if he doesn't talk down to me, the words aren't going to enter my head."

Leila started to cry, and Jerome stuttered something incomprehensible. Selma opened her mouth to speak, but just as quickly closed it and sat back in silence. She was right. They needed to hash it out between themselves.

From my position, neither viewpoint seemed 100%. And there was no way I was going to leave them be without saying so.

"Jerome," I said. "Your tone comes from constantly trying to overcompensate for the fact that you feel disliked. And Leila, your reaction to that tone is exaggerated because you dislike how his existence interferes with what you had with your mum before Jerome arrived."

Jerome and Leila both stared in opposite directions in silence.

"Jerome, other than what Leila has just said," I said, cringing at the phoniness in my voice. But it was what Selma wanted, and after the incident with the peacock in the alley, I felt it best to stick to the script. "What aspects of yourself do you feel Leila dislikes?"

Jerome scoffed. "Are you trying to set me up for failure here? It's Leila's irrational behavior that we're trying to find a solution for, not mine!"

Leila grabbed her bag and stormed out of the house.

Selma cried again.

I bit my bottom lip as the silence hummed in my ears. I'd had another an idea.

Before putting this idea forward, Eve, I decided to call it a night. I needed time to investigate whether it was possible first. So when I returned home, I called customer services at PremsBank.

"Um, hi, I was wondering if you could help me clear up a rumor." After a lifetime of telling the brutal truth without a single hitch, I was getting surprisingly good at this lying thing.

"Certainly, ma'am." The woman's voice sounded like a cartoon mouse.

"Is it against the law," I said, dragging out the last syllable, "for a man to track down the children born from his donor sperm?"

"That all depends on whether the mother signed the release form or not, ma'am."

"Release form? I don't remember being given one of those to sign when I was there."

"Yes, sorry, this document was recently introduced because a lot of donors were inquiring about their offspring.

The original contract stated that they were not permitted to obtain that information if the mother chose not to marry them. The law has recently changed, however, due to a public poll revealing that the majority of the Globe's females were not against the idea of their sperm donor connecting with their child."

"Right, so when did this law go live?" I asked, hope bubbling up inside me like a chemical reaction.

"Just three years ago, ma'am."

"So any mother that was inseminated over the last three years could potentially have signed such a release form?"

"That is correct, ma'am."

"Okay, so how do I go about finding where a male friend of mine's sperm went, and whether the women it went to signed release forms?"

"I'm afraid you can't just find that out, ma'am. There is a series of forms that need to be filled out. By the donor himself. And there is a fee."

"How long does it take for the paperwork to be issued and assessed?" I closed my eyes, imploring the universe to give me good news for a change. I didn't dare ask what the fee was yet.

"It varies ma'am. It can sometimes take days, and sometimes months. Especially if there are any discrepancies. Some women change their mind when they are contacted, and if they do, they are not legally bound to abide by the release form. We contact them here, from PremsBank, to guarantee their privacy and safety. And only if they agree to meet do we give the donor their details."

This whole thing was beginning to sound like a big joke to make some extra Sats.

"So, then what's the point of the release form?" I asked.

"It simply gives donors the legal opportunity to make contact and request a meeting."

"But we don't have time to navigate the red tape on this."
My tone had grown quite aggravated now and I was on the
verge of crossing a line.

"Excuse me, ma'am?"

I realized I'd used an obsolete term I'd learned from my
parents. The customer service representative must have
thought I was nuts. "My friend doesn't have much time. He
hasn't received the Letter and he only has a little over a
month to find happiness before he turns 40.0."

"My deepest condolences, ma'am."

"Thank you. But the thing is, this might save him. Is there
any way to sidestep the rules?" I knew I was pushing my
luck here. Governor Jacobson doesn't allow his citizens to
skip a single step in a documented process unless they 'work
with the bluebird,' whatever that meant.

"Ma'am, what you're asking is illegal. I'd also like to remind
you that all conversations are recorded at this facility to
help with the training of new recruitments."

I took a deep breath. There had to be another way to obtain
this information. And then I remembered the guy that
sold Jerome the cigars. How he had no family left and did
anything he pleased because he didn't care what happened
to him. Maybe he could take a few risks and find a few loop-
holes to obtain this information for Jerome. But Eve ... how
to get in touch?

"I apologize. Thank you for your time."

"Thank y—" I hung up before she could give me her
'die happy, live happier' spiel. It made me want to throw
up every time I heard it. Especially since it no longer just
sounded like a catchy slogan.

The next morning at the bakery I told Selma my idea and
she phoned the cigar guy, Hector, right there and then. It
turned out that he was able to acquire the documents for

his "Koumbaro"—as Selma said he liked to call him—in less than a week. Even better, he'd bring them straight to Selma and Jerome's house the following weekend, along with a complimentary box of cigars.

"Jerome must taste the Gurkha Black Dragons," he'd said. "At least once before he turns lethal."

WATCH

"**K**oumbaro, mah man!" Hector strutted in and slammed a pile of manila folders and a luxury box of cigars onto the kitchen table. "I got ya this. And I got ya this." Which one ya wanna open first, mate?"

Jerome smiled and opened his arms wide for a hug. They hugged like guys hug—afraid to show true affection, but also unable to hold back the affection, resulting in a mumble, a slap on the back, a sniff, and a straightening of the collar when they're done.

"Good to see you, Hec, really good to see you. It's been too long."

"Yeah, mate. Maybe three or four years? That last box of cigars I got ya been burned yet?"

"There's one left. I can't bring myself to smoke it. I seem to have attached a weird sentimental value to it."

Hector raised his eyebrows and scratched his bristly chin. He shook his head and said, "Mate, life's too short. Life's too short, mate."

"You can say that again. Looks like I've got a month to live." Jerome uttered this as if he was talking about something as trivial as a golf date.

"Nah, mate. Don't say that, mate." Hector jutted his chin toward the manila folders on the table. "Word has it these pussies'll sort you out, pronto."

"Yeah? I'm not sure. Selma is adamant I give it a go, but I feel like a bit of a loser, you know? Like it's just going to get me even more depressed seeing all the kids that are biologically mine and knowing I'll never get the chance to meet them. It's useless in my mind. But, yeah, I'll try it. I'll try anything for Selma. Sorry, Hec, I'm babbling. Take a seat."

Jerome pulled out a kitchen chair and gestured for Hector to sit down. He sat and opened the box of cigars. He lifted one out from the left side of the box, held it to his nose, then sniffed and sighed with pleasure.

"Wanna have a few tokes?" Hector said with a wink.

Jerome smiled like a guilty little boy.

Hector removed the bands from the cigar and handed it to Jerome to give it a good once over before smoking it. The wrapper was void of veins and shone from the oils under the kitchen light. Jerome too sniffed it. The sharp barnyard smell was typically a bit sour, but not unpleasantly so. He took a moment to feel how firmly packed it was. No hard or soft spots tarnished its perfect, even appearance. After letting himself get lost in the pleasure of looking at it, he handed it back to Hector to cut and light.

Hector groaned with deep pleasure as he took the first toke, then handed it back to Jerome. The smoke was of a medium body with a buttery flavour, enriched with a semi-sour peppery finish.

"Now this is bliss," said Jerome with a chuckle. "Screw SLP." He hung his head.

"Hec, you know what my father told me?"

"What'd he tell ya?"

"That I survived cancer against the worst odds I've ever heard of." Jerome cracked up laughing.

Hector chuckled a little, but Jerome didn't stop.

Then they both laughed hysterically.

"Did you lace these with weed?" Jerome asked with a cough. Tears streamed down his cheeks.

"Nah, mate," Hector said. "But it sounds like you could have done with some."

"Hec," Jerome said, then licked his lips. "I feel fucking hopeless. My emotions are tangled together so much that I feel like I'm going to choke on them."

Hector took the cigar from Jerome's fingers and rested it in the ashtray to let it extinguish itself.

"Koumbaro, I know this place you're at is total shit. But look at all the people around ya, people who give a damn. You won't be forgotten, mate."

Jerome laughed through his nose and punched Hector on the shoulder as a gesture of thanks.

"And you know what else I think, mate?" Hector said.

"What?"

"I knah I'm not the wisest bloke on the Globe, mate, but have you ever thought that SLP ain't all it's cracked up to be? Or maybe it doesn't even exist, yahnah? I mean, yeah, there are all these stories and shit. It sounds legit. But it could be all made up to get us into line, yahnah? I mean, have you ever heard about what it's like over there, mate? From the horse's mouth like?"

Jerome shook his head and frowned. "Come to think of it, no."

"And what about all those glass jars of blue shadows and shit? What if they're just smoke bombs and food dye?" Hector snorted. "Ya ever thoughta that? What if it's all just total bullshit like? To give the people a logical reason why they're cutting down the peeps so the Globe doesn't explode, yahnah? What if—"

"Hec?" Jerome said, grinning from ear to ear.

"Yeah mate?"

"You really believe all this crap you're saying?"

Hector laughed and slammed his fist on top of the manila folders and said, "I could've got ya all this on a stick, but I decided I wanted to be all gangsta 'n' shit."

Jerome couldn't help but laugh. "I wouldn't expect any less from you."

Hector pulled out a random folder from the middle of the pile and flipped open the cover.

"Pshh. Koumbara, this one is *hot.*" Hector spun it round so it stood the right way up for Jerome to see. "Call 'er now, I want to listen to 'er *purr.*"

Jerome knocked his knuckles on the tabletop. "Come on, Hec. This is, uh, private."

Hector screwed up his mouth and nodded. "Yeah. I get it. No worries, mate. Ya want me to uh, yahnah, fuck off?"

Jerome hesitated for a moment. "I really don't mean to kick you out after you've helped me, but if you don't mind," Jerome said. "I'm really sorry. I've had a long day, and—"

"Nah, mate. No explanation necessary. You enjoy those Black Dragons, ya 'ear?"

Jerome shook Hector's hand. "I owe you."

Hector moved his mouth like he was chewing on a tooth-pick. "You don't owe me shit, mate. But ya do owe yourself."

Jerome and Hector released their handshake. Hector nodded a goodbye and stepped backward into the hall, staring at Jerome as if it was the last time they were ever going to speak.

"Call me if ... before... yahnah ..." Hector leaned his shoulder against the door frame and, still looking Jerome square in the eye, called out a farewell to Selma, told her not to waste her time getting up, and that he could show himself out.

She called out, "Filakia!" from her bedroom. Hector teared up.

"Hec, you're not crying are you?" Jerome said.

"Nah mate," Hector said. "Greeks don't cry."

He disappeared into the hall.

Jerome remained, staring at his feet as the front door slammed shut. He sat down with his eyes closed, motionless, waves of silence surrounding his chair.

"Greeks don't cry," he whispered to himself, as a tear escaped and slid down his cheek.

DEATHCARE OBSERVATION #396, NEURAL OSCILLATION REGISTRY NO. 94793475934857

The next morning Jerome stared at the manila folders on the kitchen table while his coffee brewed. Selma approached from behind and wrapped her arms around his waist.

"Did you have a nice time last night?" she whispered, her cheek pressed between his shoulder blades.

"It was nice to see him again," Jerome said.

"That's good." Selma didn't let go. Instead, she hugged him tighter and buried her face into his back. "I love you," she said, turning Jerome around to face her.

"I'm so sorry, Sma." The last few months of Jerome's misbehavior seemed to have hit him square in the face.

Selma frowned. "For?"

"For everything I've done lately. For being so hard to live with. I'm surprised you haven't *told* me to give up yet." Hector's comment about Greeks not crying made him think about how strong that man had been all his life. He'd never given in to the system, and had simultaneously found a way to live his life to the fullest, no matter the consequences. Jerome wished he didn't care so much about consequences and more about the now. But now it was too late, and the consequences were affecting the now. There was nowhere else to run or hide or escape. It was time to face reality.

"Jome, I—" Selma pulled her hair back so hard it stretched the corners of her eyes. She took a deep breath and uttered the rest of her sentence in tears. "I have something to tell you."

Jerome placed both his hands on the edge of the kitchen counter with a sigh. "I suppose I should have expected a curveball." He looked down and poured his coffee. Strong and black. Whatever it was that Selma had done, he deserved it. He told himself to be kind, because she had done nothing but exactly that for him, despite all the terrible things he'd done to her.

Selma took a seat at the table and organized the manila folders into a neat pile.

"I can't keep secrets anymore. They're eating me up inside."

Jerome nodded, bracing himself to be heartbroken.

"Icasia isn't an aspiring writer, Jome."

Jerome turned around and leaned his backside against the counter. Relieved, he smirked, lifted his mug of coffee to his lips and sipped. "I didn't think she was," he said. "Don't worry. I can see you're fond of her. Whoever she is, I don't care. She's been a wonderful friend to you—to all of us. And you needed that. So, it's okay. Don't worry, ok—"

"Jome, I …" Selma interrupted. "I kissed her."

Jerome didn't react. He *couldn't* react. His whole body froze.

"And I liked it."

"And the stones just keep coming," Jerome said with a click of his tongue. For a short moment he stared across the room, expressionless, and for the first time in his life, he understood why his father might have preferred to appear cold and heartless. Controlling how emotions affect behavior seemed like an honorable choice in a situation like this. Especially since he didn't really have the right to be hurt.

Jerome sat opposite Selma at the table and cupped his hands over hers. He swallowed, cleared his throat, and smiled.

"Are you falling for her?" Jerome asked, with a hint of amusement in his voice.

"Jome, this isn't a joke."

Jerome dropped the smile to prove he was serious. But he couldn't help but think it funny. The image of his tall, skinny, sensible redhead wife kissing a short, stocky pretend-writer-type was hilarious to him. "It wasn't a joke question, Sma."

They stared at each other in silence for a moment.

"Should I take that to mean yes?" Jerome asked.

Selma shook her head. "Not entirely."

"What do you mean by that?" Now Jerome was a little worried.

"I mean I may have fallen for her a little bit, but I promise you it's nothing compared to how I feel about you, Jome. I really need you to understand that."

Jerome leaned back in his chair, put his hands on the back of his head and sighed.

"I knew you'd be upset," Selma said, shaking her head and looking into her lap. "I'm so sorry."

"Sma, it hurts, but it's really nothing compared to what you've had to put up with from me."

Selma nodded almost inconspicuously, but didn't make eye contact.

"Look at me, Sma," Jerome said in a gentle voice.

She lifted her head, and black mascara tears streamed down her cheeks. Jerome leaned over and dabbed them away with his thumbs.

"If I live, let's start over, okay?"

Selma wiped her eyes with the heels of her hands. "Okay."

Jerome jutted his chin toward the manila folders on the table. "You call half and I call half?" He winked. "The first woman to accept, we arrange to meet as soon as possible. And let's forget about everything that happened before today. Deal?"

"Absolutely," Selma said taking the top half of the folders and hugging them to her chest. "Anything for my Jome."

DEATHCARE CLOSING SESSION, NEURAL OSCILLATION REGISTRY NO. 9781925965605

"**M**r. Beyett." Phyvwonoh squinted and licked his lips. "This is your last session with us, I'm afraid. I've just been notified that you are, to quote directly from the memo, 'a lost cause'." Thankfully due to this diagnosis it will not be registered on my record as a failed case, and I may keep my job." Phyvwonoh paused. *I want the man to squirm.* "This is great news, is it not, Mr. Beyett?"

Jerome, having resigned himself to the fact that the next few weeks would be his last, put his hands behind his head, lifted his legs onto the couch and laid down with a chuckle.

"Well, good for you, Phy." He sensed that Phyvwonoh was seeking an outburst, a confrontation. But Jerome was done with outbursts. From now on he wouldn't give satisfaction to anyone other than himself and the people he cared about. "Any chance I can take a look at this room without the cloud simulation?"

Phyvwonoh sighed and shook his head. "I suppose it's not against the rules, so I shall oblige, Mr. Beyett." Phyvwonoh reached into the air above his head and typed a code into an invisible keypad. Keys clicked and the clouds faded. To Jerome's surprise, more than clouds subsided. The furniture, the decor, and even the comfort of the couch Jerome lay on disappeared. He glanced around the entire room now covered with a Chroma Key green screen. Phyvwonoh sat on a green box made from thin wooden slats, and Jerome sat on the same thing, except wider. And since the simulation disappeared, the hard surface dug into his back.

"You can turn it back on now, Phy." Jerome winced as he adjusted his position.

"As you wish." Phyvwonoh typed a code above his head again. The previous setup reappeared, including the comfort of the couch. "Satisfied?"

Jerome shrugged, adamant not to show surprise. "So what the hell is wrong with *real* furniture?"

"I shall let you in on a little secret, Mr. Beyett," Phyvwonoh said tapping his nose. "We have a very large database of assorted design elements, which are then custom assembled to enhance each individual patient's therapy experience according to their likes and dislikes."

"Right, okay. So what made you think that hovering clouds would float my boat? Surely you'd have had more success treating me in a fabricated prison cell." Jerome couldn't resist playing now. He had to leave his last therapy session with a bang.

Phyvwonoh frowned and lifted his index finger to his lips in contemplation. Jerome thought the mannerism looked feigned. In fact, he wouldn't be surprised if Phyvwonoh *was* a robot like he'd originally thought. No matter what the blue suits said about transparency, he was sure they would not reveal this. DeathCare Therapy from a robot? The people would completely lose faith.

"What makes you say that, Mr. Beyett?"

"Because I probably would have hated being here, and I'd have done everything I could not to ever have to come back?"

"Mr. Beyett, do I really have to remind you that you hated being here anyway?"

"No." Jerome pinched the bridge of his nose. "Right."

"Moving on." Phyvwonoh handed Jerome an envelope. "When you leave today, please sign this document and hand it to the receptionist on your way out."

"What is it?"

"A declaration of acceptance, Mr. Beyett."

Jerome laughed. "And what happens if I don't sign it?"

"Your death inducement will be treated as a hostile case and your family will not be permitted to attend."

Jerome stared at Phyvwonoh trying not to express his surprise. He couldn't believe this. Hostile case? Who did they think he was? His soul hadn't even been annihilated yet and he was already being treated like a body. With a straight face, he folded the envelope in half and slipped it into his back pocket.

"Mr. Beyett, if you do not object to my asking ... how do you intend to spend your last few weeks on the Globe?"

"I haven't finished fighting yet," Jerome said, staring out through the fake window at the fake scenery and the fake weather.

"What on the Globe do you mean? It's over. There is not enough time to find success in a career. You do know that, don't you, Mr.Beyett?"

"Well, you'll probably laugh, practically being attached to the establishment at the hip, but Selma and I believe that there is more to finding happiness than achieving a career goal."

Phyvwonoh squinted and nodded. Again. "Go on, Mr. Beyett."

Jerome considered how to word his thoughts so as not to

give away that Hector, or anyone else, had illegally obtained the contact information of who was impregnated with his sperm. "Yesterday Selma and I received a phone call from a woman named Clara. She has a son named Ben. Ben is my biological son, and Clara wondered if we might like to get acquainted with each other."

Phyvwonoh ran his tongue along his front teeth with a loud sucking noise as he stared into Jerome's eyes with great skepticism.

"I find it hard to believe that this woman was able to obtain your contact information. I am tempted to investigate whether there was a security breech, Mr. Byett."

Jerome's heart beat in his throat.

"But," Phyvwonoh added, "Perhaps it would be useless. No security alarms went off. And if your information was illegally obtained, you are only one man. A man who shortly will no longer exist. I will let it go." Phyvwonoh smacked his lips. "I'm sorry to say this, but I don't see how that is going to help you, Mr. Beyett."

"It doesn't matter what you believe, Phy. What matters is what *I* believe."

"And what, may I ask, do you believe, Mr. Beyett?"

Jerome smiled and remembered what his father had.

"Phy?"

"Yes, Mr. Beyett?"

"I believe in love."

DEATHCARE OBSERVATION #402, NEURAL OSCILLATION REGISTRY NO. 94793475934857

Jerome arrived home with hope in his heart. As he entered his house he gazed at the family photos on the wall by the door. Selma in her blue-black wedding dress and bright orange lipstick and hair, and him in his bright orange tuxedo and blue-black tie and shoes, their arms linked, smiles extending the entire width of their faces, and the fellow at the far right in the bright green jumper who decided it would be a good idea to photo-bomb every professional wedding photo they had commissioned. They didn't care, it added a certain something.

He admired Leila as a beautiful little girl, with hair so blonde and frizzy they couldn't find a single product to tame it, playing in the sand at Bit Point Beach. She was smiling at the camera. And Jerome was behind the camera. There were some days when he really thought she'd started to love him. He *did* love her, but there had always been a layer of film between them, an inseparable barrier that stopped them becoming close. He believed that meeting her so late in childhood had a negative impact on their ability to bond. If he'd met her as a baby, then maybe things might have turned out better between them.

He removed his coat and hung it on the coat rack. Two female voices, and another voice that sounded like that of a young boy, traveled down the hallway from the kitchen. He assumed Icasia and Abel were visiting. He strutted down the hallway toward the arched entrance of the kitchen fully prepared to ignore whatever inkling of embarrassment remained from the unfortunate incident behind The Ambrosial Inn.

But it wasn't them.

It was Clara and Ben from the only manila folder that produced positive results.

Clara smiled, stood up and held out her hand for Jerome to shake. Jerome stepped forward hesitantly and shook it. He wanted to speak, but his tongue was tied. Thankfully Clara, a charming young woman with wavy waist-length chestnut hair, broke the silence.

"It's lovely to meet you, Jerome. I honestly couldn't believe it when your wife called me yesterday. I think it was fate. Because I'd been wondering what you might be like, and was wishing that my sperm donor had been single so that we could have been a biological family. It's pretty rare nowadays." Clara blushed. She glanced at Selma and then at her little boy who had buried his head into the back of her knees. Selma smiled and touched her gently on the shoulder. Clara cleared her throat and looked down at Ben. "Anyway, this is Ben. Your son."

Jerome knelt down so that his eyes were level with Ben's. His hands trembled and his tongue stuck to the roof of his mouth. "Hello there, little fella. Please don't hide. I promise I won't tickle you."

Ben giggled and exposed one eye from behind Clara's knees. Jerome's heart fluttered a little in his chest. Their eyes were practically identical. Dark brown and a little slanted at the outer edges.

Jerome winked at him and held out his hand. Clara said, "Come on honey. Please don't be shy. He's your daddy and he loves you." Clara winked at Jerome to make sure he knew she was saying it to make Ben feel safe. But the way Jerome's heart was beating in his ears with such a depth of need made him believe it may not have been far from the truth.

Ben giggled again and stepped out from behind Clara's knees. He hesitated for a moment, but then launched himself into Jerome's arms like a rocket.

Clara and Selma laughed as Jerome lifted is son—his real-life biological son—into his arms, hugged him and spun him around. He breathed in the wholesome scent of a little man that was a true part of his core. Ben's hair smelled like fresh mint, and his skin like baby powder.

He couldn't believe it. He was holding his *son*.

He was holding his *own son*.

Ben whispered in Jerome's ear. "Hello, Daddy."

Jerome's heart melted and a couple of tears slipped down his left cheek. He put Ben on the kitchen table so he could look him in the eye, and said, "Hello ... son."

LISTEN

By the time Clara and Ben left that afternoon, they had all decided to remain in each other's lives. Selma and Jerome decided not to tell Clara and Ben about Jerome's predicament yet. There was no point in conjuring negative feelings when he still had three weeks left to live. I'm sure you agree, Eve. Selma did call me, though, and told me all about the meeting. She couldn't stop laughing from excitement, and felt positive that Jerome had made a breakthrough. She told me she'd called the Neural Oscillation Registry to ask how long it typically took to receive a letter if someone's oscillation had reached gamma frequency, and they said anywhere between one and twenty-four hours. She asked if I would come over for an early dinner and wait with them. She was almost certain he'd receive one that night. Eve, I couldn't refuse.

After dinner we sat at the kitchen table pretty much listening to the clock tick. To pass the time we played cards, read each other interesting articles from our Comms, shared a Black Dragon cigar between us, and drank two bottles of red wine. Selma talked about her ideas for the bakery and how she could teach Jerome how to bake—just a few basic things—so it could become a solid family business. She said she didn't need to do this on her own anymore. That she was ready to share it. She wanted Jerome on board. He was extremely keen, but kept reminding Selma to not keep her hopes up.

"But why not?" Selma said with a slight slur.

"I think it's a great idea," I said. "And there's no reason why you shouldn't think positively about all this. It sounds like this afternoon went extremely well." Of course, I had doubts, but I had to remain positive. For them. But, Eve, something just felt ... off.

"Thank you. Yes," Selma said with conviction. "That's the attitude you need, Jome. Take a few lessons from the writer here." Selma winked at Jerome. Right then I knew that he knew the truth, and my stomach sank. His gaze shifted over my face as fast as a vampire on the hunt.

I tried to ignore the growing hollowness in my chest. It wasn't the time to put a downer on their hopeful mood. But what would happen now? I thought. If Jerome received the Letter, and started working at the bakery, would I end up back on the street looking for another place to tat? The thought made me want to vomit.

The clock chimed midnight.

"When's the twenty-four-hour mark?" I asked, after hours of listening to Selma and Jerome chatter like a couple on a first date.

"Three o'clock tomorrow after—" Their Comm rang and jolted Selma upright. "Sorry." She looked at the caller ID. It was Gary. She handed the Comm to Jerome, whose voice croaked when he answered.

He held the phone to his ear, and then closed his eyes and winced. Though he said nothing but "okay" three or four times throughout the whole conversation, he nodded a lot, with his hand on his forehead.

He hung up, handed the Comm to Selma and sighed. Selma shrugged in question.

"They've pushed forward Dad's death inducement a couple of weeks due to 'lack of resources.' Whatever that means."

"What?" Selma said. "To when?"

"Tomorrow."

There were hundreds of rooms at the Anima Cemetery in which death inducements took place. Naively believing that happiness was a given as long as you lived by the Book, people followed the rules and believed nothing would ever go wrong, despite the inducements being nothing like they were portrayed on the inTel. For one, the offspring and other relatives were not standing around the induced parent drinking champagne in celebration of 'life,' while the parent's soul slowly and happily passed into its Transition Grave.

Yet the statistics were wonderful. And they were available to the public. 99.5% of the Globe's documented citizens successfully transitioned into the Second Life Phase. And that wasn't a lie. Remember, Eve, when Norate, from PremsBank, said "There are no secrets here?" Well, that was true. But information was only given out if it was asked for. And no one thought to—including me—submit an official request asking what 'documented' actually meant. I would soon discover that 'documented' referred to people who were receiving health benefits from the government. People like me and Abel and Hector and anyone who chose to live independently as much as possible from the system, were not 'documented citizens.' Now I was never able to find out exactly how many of the Globe's citizens weren't documented, but I'm guessing there were enough to significantly lower the percentage, and it was therefore decided to use this truth to deceive.

So people were very rarely worried about a death induce-ment. They had gotten used to the idea that the people passing on were going to a better place. And this made everything all right.

But it wasn't all right. Not to us. Not since this devastating change in the law. And I wouldn't have been surprised if there were a million families experiencing exactly the same thing that Selma and Jerome were experiencing. And they were all probably too naive to challenge it, or too afraid to think outside the box. Fear is a powerful thing—and some-times a comfort.

Selma, Jerome, Leila, and I followed the bluebird into the Inducement Chamber. It looked like Gary's garage. His place of comfort and calm. The bluebird perched on the windowsill next to a little bronze chest that could fit into my pocket.

Gary cried and held Jerome in his arms, standing in the middle of the chamber for a good twenty minutes next to a box of tools. Selma and Leila held hands and stood against the back wall. They weren't crying, but the color had disap-peared from their faces. I stood a meter away from them, unsure how much I should interfere. I didn't even know what I was doing there, but Selma and Jerome had insisted I come. Selma held out her free hand and asked me to join them. I took her hand, which was clammy and cold, and squeezed it in sympathy.

My heartbeat increased at the thought of Abel being in this position one day, watching me be induced and knowing that it was the complete and utter end of his mother. I started to cry and choke on my own breath, wondering whether it was just easier to be naive. Perhaps it was easier to accept the rules we were given, to abide by them 100% and avoid the heavy black burden of knowledge.

I hung my head to hide my tears, but Leila saw them. She

let go of her mother's hand, came to my side and squeezed the back of my neck. She said, "I know what you're thinking. I'm sorry."

After half an hour, the Inducement Practitioner entered the chamber and folded his hands together in front of his chest like he was about to pray.

"Hello. My name is Asten. Welcome. Before we begin, I'd like to explain the procedure and the logistics to you so that there are no surprises."

Jerome and Gary let go of each other, wiped away their tears, and stood with their heads down and their hands folded behind their backs. It looked like they were both about to be cuffed and hanged.

"Mr. Beyett—"

"Gary. Please call me Gary. And I think we know the drill."

Asten nodded. "I must explain the procedure. It's protocol, I'm afraid. A little like the police must recite your rights."

Gary stood in silence and stared at Asten. After a moment, he proceeded.

"Gary will be placed in a horizontal position on the floor, as per his wishes, so as to avoid his body's collapse when his soul is extracted. His soul will be extracted when we administer the hydroatmoxide. The extracted soul will then be drawn toward Gary's Transition Grave by a spiritual force, which we call the Arc. The Arc is produced naturally at birth and hovers above you throughout your life, so that in the event that you die suddenly, it is there to lead your soul toward its Transition Grave. All Transition Graves are produced within ten days of one's birth to mimic the genetic code of one's body so that the soul is able to maintain a sense of belonging. You will not see the soul's release when Gary loses consciousness. It is only visible once inside its Transition Grave. The reason for this is that a soul becomes

transparent when it comes in contact with the Globe's atmosphere. But research suggests that it is, in fact, blue when it
is inside you. You may visit Gary's soul at any time after his
inducement, but be sure to make an appointment as this is
a very busy time of year for us. In addition, once Gary's soul
is captured in his Transition Grave, Gary's body will evaporate immediately. Before we proceed, I would like you to let
me know if witnessing the evaporation will be distressing to
any of you. If so, we can arrange for a video of the event to
be captured should you wish to see it at a later stage when
you feel ready. That is all. Would everyone like to remain in
the chamber?"

Everyone except Leila nodded. She burst into tears and
requested to leave.

Asten led her toward the exit, but on passing, Jerome
grabbed her arm and said, "Wait. Please." Leila shook her
head and tried to yank her arm away, but Jerome wouldn't
let go. "I know life is scary. Life will always be scary. And
many things beyond today are going to make you cry,"
Jerome said, moving his hand to cup her cheek. He lowered
his voice a little, and continued, "But sweetheart, if you
don't find the courage to face the things that hurt you, you
will never find the motivation to love and enjoy the things
that make you happy."

Leila looked at her feet, gulped, and wiped away her tears.
She hugged Jerome around his waist. Jerome hugged her
back, kissed her on the top of her head and whispered,
"Please stay. Please don't hide from life. Don't start the rollercoaster of what will eventually lead to my demise."

The room fell silent and Asten wiped away an invisible
tear. Leila didn't say a word, but she stayed, and held
Jerome's hand as Gary lowered himself onto the mattress
on the floor.

Asten massaged Gary's arms so that they were not rigidly squeezing his torso. The bluebird chirped, opened the little bronze chest with its beak and pulled out a thin glass cylinder filled with what looked like a sample from a cloud. It hovered next to Asten, with the cylinder grasped firmly in its beak.

Asten knelt down beside Gary and asked Jerome to kneel down on the other side.

"Hold your father's hand, Jerome. I am going against protocol here, but I am well aware of your situation, and I could not possibly go through with this inducement without offering my sincerest condolences and genuine wishes of good luck. I very much hope you receive the Letter today." Asten squeezed Gary's hand, and Jerome squeezed the other.

"Thank you," Jerome said. "That means a lot. I know you're just doing your job. I blame Jacobson."

Asten cleared his throat and glanced toward the corner of the ceiling. I looked up to see what was there. It was a small camera.

Gary, with his eyes closed, grabbed Asten's arm and squeezed it so hard I could see his knuckles turn white. "I trust this moment will be considered an innocent misjudgment resulting from my son's grief, and that he won't be walking out of here with a summons to court for slander."

Asten's breath shuddered as he inhaled. "Of course, Gary. Nothing of the sort will happen. I know who you are."

Gary nodded in thanks and turned to Jerome and said, "I have faith in you, son. And I love you, no matter what."

Jerome rested his forehead on Gary's chest and sobbed. His shoulders moved up and down while Asten took the hydroatmoxide from the bluebird's beak and released it into the atmosphere above Gary's nose.

"Take a deep breath, Gary. It will only take a moment before you feel like you are floating on clouds."

Gary breathed in and his chest rose. When he breathed out again, he vanished.

I closed my eyes in comprehending silence and a thick sense of disbelief. I crossed my fingers behind my back, hoping that Jerome would receive the Letter that day, so that at the very least Gary's death would not be a real one. I thought to myself that I would do anything right then to gift this family happiness, because that would mean that I'd have hope too. But I would soon realize that my biggest obstacle in life was that I always sought a reward or recognition for a good deed. And my good intentions were tainted by that. Doing something good for someone—*truly* good for someone—meant not thinking about myself at all.

Jerome didn't receive the Letter that day.

At Selma's house after the inducement, we all stood in the lounge room staring at a photo of Jerome's parents in the very center of the mantel.

No one made a sound.

Words no longer made sense.

Selma decided to keep the bakery closed during the last weeks of Jerome's life so that they could stay home and spend some quality time together. Leila visited every day, and even though her relationship with Jerome wasn't perfect, she decided it would be the right thing to do to put her feelings aside and be there for him and her mother.

Selma and Jerome opened a Crypto account for me and deposited 300,000,000 Sats into it. Jerome said with a wink, "Make it last or find a job. Your call." I had to laugh. I knew it was his way of saying thank you, and I appreciated that.

I was feeling quite sorry for myself, missing the bakery and Selma's company, but I stayed out of their hair and gave them space. I knew it wasn't my place to visit unless I was invited. I *was* invited a few times, and on one of those occasions I didn't go because I couldn't stop crying that day. All I kept thinking about was Gary's death inducement, and how awful that kind of future was going to be for Abel. I knew I was a lost cause. There was no fixing this for me. But depression crept up on me like a sun shower. Unexpected. Irrational. Strangely nostalgic and hopeful.

I knew my parents weren't worried about the SLP because they believed that people only had one life. They'd made it very clear to me from the first day I started to comprehend words to ignore the Book and live for myself and myself only. Of course, when Abel was born, I started to live for us both. I knew that whether I believed what my parents believed or not really made no difference at that point in time, but I'd always held the opinion that everybody should keep an open mind regardless. Without an open mind, there is no door for a pleasant surprise to enter through.

One day, about a week before Jerome's scheduled annihilation, Selma asked me to pick up some ingredients from her bakery so she could bake a cake for Jerome's farewell party.

When I arrived back home, my next-door neighbor, Missy, who would always bang on the wall to complain about the smallest noise coming from our squat, was sitting on my couch. Abel was on the floor crashing a toy truck into a toy car over and over and over, making sound effects that resembled a plane falling from the sky. Missy wasn't the kindest soul on the Globe, but I knew she had a good heart underneath her aloof exterior.

"Put those bags down, love, and come sit." She patted the seat next to her.

"Where are my parents?" I looked around the room, and through the door into our bedroom, but they were nowhere to be seen.

"Well, see love, that's the fing. They're not here."

I raised my eyebrows and scoffed, wondering if this was some kind of joke.

"They can't have just disappeared." I frowned.

"No, love," Missy said. She rubbed my knee with a wince. "But the fing is they've been taken to St. Jacob's 'ospital. They was hit by a truck, love. Out shopping for a little sumfink for your bakery friend. Abel was brought back here by the lady what runs the fruit shop just down the road."

My throat grew dry and I almost gagged when I tried to swallow. I glanced at Abel, who was still crashing his toys together. It suddenly dawned on me why he was doing that, and I jumped out of my seat and kicked his toys out of the way.

"Abel. Abel! Look at me. Are you okay?"

Abel nodded, but I checked him over anyway. Stripped him bare right there in the middle of the room, much to Missy's surprise. Not a single mark, cut, or bruise on his body, but he wouldn't speak.

"Abel. Talk to me. What happened?"

Silence.

I looked at Missy, sitting in silence on the couch with her hands folded in her lap.

"Thank you, Missy. Thank you for looking after him." My voice shook and I burst into tears. Missy stood and walked to my side. She rested her hand on my upper back and offered me a tissue. I took it and blew my nose.

"You should go to the 'ospital, love."

"But what about Abel? He's seen and been through enough." I held my hand to my mouth to dampen the wail that escaped.

"He's all right here with me, love. You go. It's okay. You ain't got nuffink to worry 'bout. As of last week, I am a great great grandmother. I know a fing or two about young boys."

"Oh, thank you!" I wailed and flung my arms around her shoulders. She stood there like a lamp post, but I didn't care. I kissed Abel on the head, hugged him tightly to my chest, whispered "I love you" over and over in his ear until I finally managed to pull myself away and grab my bag.

I ran.

I ran and I realized that I didn't want to live my life without my parents. I loved them. I loved them so much that the thought of them not being able to live a second life ripped my heart to shreds.

I ran and I realized that I now believed. I believed in whatever it was that would help my son wake up day after day with a smile on his face, day after day without worry, without guilt, without this horrible sense that there was no true purpose to life. I was no longer a tatter. I was a believer. I believed that the purpose of life was whatever we wanted it to be—whatever we made it. Happiness was in our own hands, and that was a gift. It was a gift because we had a choice. It may have been the only real choice we were entitled to anymore on this emotionally volatile Globe.

I ran and I decided I wanted to give Abel a life of purpose, and the only way I could do that was by giving myself a purposeful life and my parents a chance at a second one.

I arrived at the hospital, puffing and gasping for air. I looked up at the plaque by the entrance of the building, trying to catch my breath. It read: *To believe in nothing is death.*

My parents' doctor said they were both in a coma, and he couldn't say for sure if they were going to wake up.

I sat between their beds holding my mother's hand in my left and my father's in my right. I spoke to them. I told them all about Selma and Jerome, and the events of the last five months and how everything leading up to this moment had helped me to make peace with myself and the Globe. But I also told them I wasn't going to stop fighting for my rights, or that I suddenly believed what the Jacobson Movement stood for. It just meant that I now had an open mind. And could educate myself without inflicting my own bias on every choice I made.

Suddenly I felt light and free. My heart could finally breathe.

And a moment later, my parents' hands were no longer in mine.

My parents ... were gone.

I stood up and looked at the empty beds in disbelief. Where had they gone? And how? And then I saw the machines had flatlined and I remembered what Asten said at Gary's inducement. Once the soul is released, the body will immediately evaporate.

I didn't cry. I couldn't cry. My tears had all been used up. I walked backwards until I reached the wall and let myself slide down it. I sat on the cold floor, staring into nothingness. No one came in to explain what had happened. No one came in to pack up the equipment or offer me their condolences. It felt like I sat there for hours, listening to the beat of my own heart, wondering how I was going to break this news to Abel, when a nurse inched open the door. He knelt down beside me, handed me an envelope, and said, "Congratulations."

It was the Letter.

My Letter.

I went home, grabbed Abel, and caught a cab to Selma's after spending a few minutes asking the nurses at the reception desk if they'd received their letters and what they had done that day or the day before. I'd had a revelation, and I needed evidence to prove it.

Their stories proved it.

I rapped on Selma's door so hard and long, but no one answered. I rapped again, and again, and again. The lights were on, so I knew they were home. A woman wearing peach flannel pajamas with waist-length chestnut hair answered the door. A little boy ran up behind her and hugged the back of her legs. I recognized who they were from Selma's description. Clara must have recognized Abel and me, because she smiled and let us in without a word.

"I'm so sorry to barge in like this so late in the evening, but I need to speak to Selma and Jerome right now."

"Of course. They said you're welcome here any time. They've missed you lately, actually."

Eve, this warmed my heart.

"Jerome has just popped out for a minute, but Selma is here. Ben, sweetie? Why don't you take Abel to see your new train set while the mums have a cup of tea, hey?"

Abel looked up at me to see if it was okay, and I nodded.

"Why don't you pop the kettle on, Icasia. I'll run upstairs and tell Selma you're here."

I was speechless at this adorable young lady's hospitality. We were probably around the same age, but she seemed so much younger than me, yet considerably more mature in the head. I managed a nod and a smile of thanks then took off my jacket and hung it on the back of a kitchen chair.

Selma walked in, her eyes all puffy and red like she'd been crying for days. I didn't ask why. I knew why.

But we did hug. And when we did I couldn't tell who was consoling who. Even though Selma didn't know what had happened that day, the hug felt like it was intended to soothe.

Clara poured the tea and joined us at the table. It felt

really strange to me, to have to talk about so many personal things in front of her, but Selma seemed relaxed about it, so I tried not to let it bother me.

I told them all about my day, and my parents, and freaking out about Abel living a life in fear. It took a great effort to curb Selma's attempts to console me for my loss, but it was important that I just get it all off my chest before telling them about my idea. Without them knowing the events of the day, the idea would seem useless. When I'd finished, I reached behind me and pulled my letter out of my jacket pocket. I unfolded it and flattened it out on the table.

Selma squinted at it as she took a sip from her mug. Then her eyes widened and lit up.

"No way!" Selma squealed and jumped out of her chair. Her jaw dropped and she held her head, fingers clutching her frizzy curls. "How Icasia? What did you do?"

I guided her back into her seat and said, "That's exactly what I'm here to tell you. I've had a bit of a revelation. It's Jerome's last shot, Selma, but I really think it will work."

Selma glanced at Clara and took a huge swig of her cold milky tea with a wince.

"Speak," Selma said with a slight growl. "I'll try anything. *He'll* try anything."

"Is it possible to have Leila give birth before Jerome's inducement?"

"Yes. We've already applied to have that done and it's been accepted."

"Good. Is Leila okay about Jerome being present at the birth?"

"Yes." Selma sighed. "I think I know where you're going with this, but it won't work. If it didn't work with Ben, why would it work with his grandchild?"

"Because with Ben, the love was one-sided. And with

Leila, the love is pretty much one-sided too. It's something he's missing in his life. I truly believe that what Jerome needs is *mutual* unconditional love. If Jerome is present at Leila's birth, and Leila doesn't object to him being the first to hold her baby, then that baby is going to connect with him as though he is a parent. That bond is sealed immediately. There's no doubt about it. And there's no doubt that Jerome is going to unconditionally love his grandchild."

Selma tutted. "If it's mutual unconditional love that's the trigger, then how do you explain your letter, or my letter, or everybody else's letter that was achieved from reaching a career milestone?"

"Because it's not the mutual love that is the trigger. It's got to be a different thing for everyone. Different things make different people happy. We're not all the same. And it's not just the trigger of happiness either. I think it's understanding yourself, and understanding what you need in order to be content, even if that's on a subconscious level. For me, I think it was to stop being so selfish all the time, and to realize that nothing is black and white. For you, I think it was because you'd finally found someone to confide in and someone to nurture who didn't judge you. I asked a couple of nurses what they were doing when they got their letters. One of them said she got hers after she had complained that if only she could get some time alone she would feel happy. So her husband paid for a weekend trip which she spent alone in a luxury resort, but the whole time she was there she said she was lonely, and all she thought about was going home again. When she did return, she said she felt a huge sense of relief holding her daughter in her arms again, and having her husband hold her in his. A couple of hours later, she received her Letter. She thought her status as a high achieving nurse was the trigger. But I told her my theory, and it was like a light flicked on in her head. She said, 'Oh my goodness. I got my letter because I had finally appreciated what was right under my very nose!' So, don't you see? They've got it all wrong, Selma. Those scientists at that stupid Neural Oscillation Registry. They've got it all wrong. They're mistaking career success as the trigger because the majority of the people on this Globe live by the Book and have good jobs. Of course, they're going to think it's material success that motivates us. They're just following the lead of history. We may have once been a materialistic species, but we're not anymore. And I hate to say it, but if there is any good that has come from the Jacobson Movement, it's that we are finally learning that we need to feed our souls rather than our bank accounts."

Selma stared at me with an open mouth—frozen in her seat.

Clara started laughing with realization. "I got my letter," she said, "after I gave a little boy on the side of the street one of Ben's toys. When I was a kid, I never shared my stuff. I wanted it all to myself." Clara grabbed my face and kissed me on the forehead, then jumped up and fetched Selma's Comm. She held it in front of her face and said, "Call him. Get him home. Now."

Selma fumbled with the Comm, holding her breath. She misdialed a couple of times, once almost dropping it, but when she pulled herself together and pressed the correct contact, there was no answer.

"Where did he go at this time of night anyway?" I asked.

"He said he needed to clear his head. He didn't say where he was going."

"You didn't ask?"

"I didn't think it was necessary. He's done this a few times and has come back in one piece. It's hardly the time to be playing the nagging wife, so I just let him be."

Clara ran down the hallway and returned with Jerome's Comm.

"I suppose we'll have to wait until he comes home on his own," Clara said. "It's really late, and I should get Ben to bed."

Selma rubbed her brow. "As much as I want to resolve this now, Leila isn't scheduled to give birth until the day after tomorrow, so we can speak to Jerome when he gets home. There's no way we can speed this up."

I nodded and looked at the boys, who had both fallen asleep on the floor surrounded by fluffy toys and building blocks.

"I'll make up the sofa bed for you and Abel," Selma said. "Don't be going back to your squat at this time of night. Not after what happened with your parents."

But then her Comm rang.

It wasn't Jerome, it was Leila.

You'll never believe it, Eve. She was in labour.

Selma rushed to Leila's squat and took her to the hospital. Clara stayed in to look after the boys. I searched for Jerome. We had to find him quickly if our plan was going to work.

Selma gave me a list of places he might be, and even though I hadn't sat behind a wheel since I was a teenager, she gave me her car.

I went to each place on the list in order of increasing distance from the hospital. But he wasn't at any of them, not even at the Anima Cemetery, which I thought would have been the most likely place.

The Anima Cemetery was the last place on my list, and I sat on the edge of the fountain and called Selma.

"I can't find him "

"No, no, no, please don't tell me that. Leila's baby is

coming, but the cord is stuck around the poor little thing's neck and she has to have a caesarean. They're rolling her into the theater now."

"I don't know what to do," I said, feeling helpless. But then it hit me. The Ambrosial Inn. The aqueduct behind it. I wouldn't blame anyone for going on a sex rampage if they only had a few days to live. "Wait, I think I know where to find him. Do everything you can to stall them, can you?"

"I'll see what I can do. Hurry!"

I hung up and jumped in the car. Started the engine, choked the gear stick, stalled it. Started it again and skidded off to The Ambrosial.

In less than a minute I was there, breaking all the road rules, I'm sure. But it was the middle of the night and the streets were empty.

Jerome was there. Standing right at the edge of the water, barefoot, his toes hanging off the edge, staring at his reflection.

I called out to him from the car before making my way over.

"Jerome! Leila's having her baby! You need to come. Now!"

Jerome shook his head and said something incomprehensible. I ran over to him and tried to pull him away from the edge, but he slapped my hand away.

"I don't want to be put down like a fucking dog in that fucking chamber in a *fucking* holographic false sense of comfort. I'd rather die on my own terms."

"What? In the aqueduct? It's not deep enough."

"But the current is strong enough to sweep me away and into the dam."

"Jerome, please. Don't you want to meet your grandchild first?"

Jerome frowned and burst into tears. "Yes, but I don't

want to be one of the first things my grandchild sees. I'm a man who failed his family. What kind of first impression of the Globe is that? I can't, okay? I just can't do it."

"Jerome, don't be ridiculous. I can't explain right now because we don't have time, but if you come now, it just might save you."

Jerome shot me a look as if I'd said the most offensive thing ever. I called Selma and handed the Comm to him. Her incomprehensible voice boomed through the sound piece—a constant storm of fuzzy noise. Jerome shook his head. Nodded. Shook his head. Said "but—" a few too many times and got cut off. Sobbed some more and hung up.

"Fine," he said. "Let's go. But I'm not doing this to save myself. I'm doing this for Leila. She said she wants me there."

I flung my arms up in the air and said, "Whatever gets you to the hospital, dude. Now get in the fucking car." There was no point pretending to be a perfectly articulate character anymore.

We arrived at the hospital and ran straight up to the theater. We weren't allowed in, so I waved through the glass to try and get Selma's attention while Jerome paced up and down behind me in the hall. Everything inside the theatre was blue, but dimmed, to make it look like nighttime. The ceiling and twinkling stars shone from above. Leila lay on the gurney, wide awake, while one doctor—one—performed a strange procedure with his hands hovering above Leila's abdomen. No machines, no nurses, just the doctor, Selma, Clara, Ben and Abel, stood by her side holding hands with their eyes closed. Their mouths moved quickly, like they were chanting something. It looked like one of the witch's cults I'd read about at the library.

I banged on the glass and got told off by a nurse walking down the hall, but I banged again anyway. A couple of security guards came running down the hallway, so I banged and yelled even louder. Just as they grabbed my arms and pulled them behind my back, Selma opened her eyes and ran to the door.

"Stop! They're with us." Selma ran to Jerome and cupped his face in her hands with a huge smile on her face. "Come."

She ran us inside the theater just as the flesh of Leila's abdomen parted on its own.

There was no blood, just the doctor's hands hovering above, controlling the procedure with his energy.

Once the abdomen was completely open, the doctor held one hand directly above the baby, with clawed fingers. He twisted his hand in the air, like he was opening a jar, and the baby eased out and upward, gracefully like a spirit rising to heaven, just enough for someone to be able to manually lift her out.

The doctor looked at Jerome, who was watching the whole thing in a trance with a slightly open mouth.

"I hear you are to be the first one to hold your granddaughter."

Jerome nodded and stepped closer to the gurney. The doctor flushed some warm liquid over the baby's head and torso. "Just ease her out as though you were lifting her out of her cot."

Jerome looked at his granddaughter's head and torso resting outside Leila's womb, on her hip. "Why isn't she crying?"

"She will. Hold her first and then I will clear her airways. She will take her first breath in your arms."

Jerome eased his granddaughter out of Leila's womb, cradled her in his arms, and gently hugged her to his chest.

He inhaled a staggered breath and started to cry like a wounded animal.

"She's a miracle, isn't she?" The doctor said. A bluebird flew down from the domed ceiling and hovered behind Jerome, whistling beautiful birdsong. Jerome's granddaughter flailed her arms and wailed.

Everyone, including me, sighed with relief and applauded. I bent down and gave Abel the biggest and longest hug I had ever given him in my life. I realized I had been so busy trying to take care of him—to feed him and keep him safe—that I hadn't paid enough attention to showing him affection. I promised myself then and there that I would do that more often.

Jerome looked up and smiled at Selma, then at me. Tears streamed down his cheeks as he mouthed, "Thank you."

I could see it in his eyes—his sparkling brown eyes—that he was happy.

The doctor circled an open hand over Leila's exposed abdomen. It joined back together and healed itself without a scar.

Leila opened her eyes and whispered Jerome's name.

Jerome approached the edge of the gurney and rested his granddaughter on her chest, and said, "Congratulations, sweetie. You have a beautiful baby girl."

Selma approached the opposite side of the gurney and stroked the baby's delicate head. "What are you going to call her, Leila?"

Leila paused for a moment, and glanced toward me. With a knowing smile, she said, "Eve. Her name is Eve. It means 'giver of life'."

"That's perfect," I said. "And it's beautiful."

I looked up at the extraordinary ceiling and the night sky

started to lighten. It was as if the sun was beginning to rise.
Four little bluebirds hovered silently above us.
One for each member of the Beyett family, I thought.
I later discovered that that was true.

DEATHCARE OBSERVATION #489, NEURAL OSCILLATION REGISTRY NO. 94793475934857

With the emotional weight lifted from his shoulders, Jerome nipped home to pick up some fresh clothes and toiletries for Leila's overnight stay in the hospital. He pulled into the driveway, finally feeling as if he could breathe again. He'd met his granddaughter, and his love for her was true. It was a feeling he had never experienced before. He didn't even care if he received a letter or not. If he died today, he would die happy, he thought.

A man in a blue suit saluted him from the front porch, then approached the car. He rapped the passenger window and stood tall.

Jerome's heart beat in his ears and the air flew from his lungs. He froze, and for a short moment he couldn't breathe.

Is this it? Are they taking me now?

"Mr. Beyett, please roll down your window."

Jerome inhaled deeply and, with a trembling hand, pressed the open button under the right edge of his seat.

The window slid down without a sound. The sun was rising and the birds were singing. A ray of gold light splashed across the face of the man in the blue suit as a lawn mower

hummed into action somewhere. Jerome realized that he
was biting the insides of his cheeks, so he loosened his jaw
and forced a smile.

This is an early collection, he thought. Like they'd done
with his father at a moment's notice.

The man slid his right hand into the left inner pocket
of his jacket. His hand paused there while he looked into
the sun and smiled subtly as it warmed his baby-smooth
complexion. "It's going to be a beautiful day, Mr. Beyett." He
pulled an envelope out of his jacket and passed it to Jerome,
who took it and held it with both hands in his lap.

"You have a nice day, Mr. Beyett," the man knocked on the
roof of the vehicle twice. Jerome watched in the rear-view
mirror as he stood by the gate and held up two fingers. A
bluebird landed on them and sang as he gently stroked the
bluebird's head, leaned in and whispered something to it.
Jerome was certain he saw the bluebird nod.

Without looking back, the man released the bluebird,
straightened his jacket, and strutted down the footpath,
whistling.

Jerome stared at the envelope in his hands. Then he
ripped it open.

Dear Jerome Beyett,

*Congratulations! You have been granted access to
a Transition Grave once you reach the age of 40.0,
and your parents, Ranita and Gary Beyett, have been
released into the Second Life Phase where they will
live in eternal harmony.*

*Please let us take the time to remind you that in order
for you to be released into the Second Life Phase, your*

daughter, *Leila Beyett, must successfully find happiness. If you are interested in providing her with a DeathCare therapist, please contact us at the number below and we'll be happy to mail you an introductory booklet free of charge.*

Thank you for cooperating with the Jacobson Movement and we wish you well in all your endeavors until the day of your death inducement.

Sincerely Yours,
Norone
Chief Executive Officer
Neural Oscillation Registry
www.nor.com

Jerome had completely forgotten about his own death inducement.

He would turn 40.0 in three days' time.

WATCH

G ary's consciousness was active. He had no idea where he was, where he had come from, or where he would end up. He lived in a soul that floated inside a galaxy of silent voices. He lived in darkness. Such darkness that his very existence seemed at the same time infinite and confined to half an inch of atmosphere surrounding the perception of his former body.

He had no idea how long he'd been floating there. It could have been years, days, or minutes. He felt like everything. The waiting. The time ... He *was* time. He was Jacobson. He was the Globe. Gary existed in his own consciousness, far from home, comfort, or reality.

Whatever such concepts were.

Was *this* reality?

Was this how he would spend eternity? Floating, wondering if time passed or stood still? Wondering if his consciousness had turned inside out? Wondering if knowing meant unknowing? Were these thoughts even his own in this darkness, which sometimes felt like light in his former heart— but only when he visualized his wife?

The vision of his wife was not even complete anymore. He saw her eyes and a very vague outline of her lips, but the rest of her shone as a light continuously morphed into clouds of mourning, uncertainty and a juxtaposed feeling of aspiration and surrender.

She was missing. He was missing. Missing the ability to comprehend.

A nothingness that did not make him feel empty.

An emptiness that did not make him feel hopeless.

A hopelessness that did not make him feel purposeless.

Because purpose existed.

But the purpose wasn't clear until he felt his wife's consciousness merge with his own.

And then it did.

Her voice echoed through his limbs, and sharp rays of light drew an outline of her body right in front of him. He glanced down and his own body also appeared, and the darkness became light, and the light become their home, and their furniture faded into existence, and dinner appeared on the table—Ranita's specialty: chicken and vegetable soup with piping hot garlic bread.

And then before he could even blink, he was sitting opposite his beloved wife, wearing a dark blue suit, eating dinner and laughing at her jokes.

For a split second, he remembered the limbo.

But then it ... vanished.

"Could you pass the salt, dear?" Gary said. "Is it your birthday today? Have I experienced a bit of a brain lapse? Something like Déjà vu?"

Ranita chewed and swallowed, resting her cutlery on the side of her plate and tilted her head. "You know, I was just thinking the same thing, dear. Is today a special occasion?"

Gary scoffed and patted his mouth with his napkin. "I think we're just getting old," he laughed.

Ranita nodded and raised her wine glass. "Here's to getting old together."

Gary clinked his glass with hers. "Absolutely. And may we enjoy every single moment of it." Gary winked and the sparkle in Ranita's eyes reminded him that the simplest things in life never failed to make him feel completely and utterly content.

"It's a good life, isn't it dear?"

"Yes," said Ranita. "And we're never going to forget it."

LISTEN

Selma laughed and cried and launched herself into Jerome's embrace as Clara and I helped tidy the kitchen after Jerome's farewell dinner. It wasn't really a big do, but I was super glad to have met the elusive cigar guy, Hector, even though he tried to hit on me right in front of Abel!

"I'm going to miss you so much, Jome," Selma said. "But I'm going to see you in SLP, so I really shouldn't complain, should I?" Selma glanced at Leila and smiled. "We're all going to miss you, I think."

"Yeah, Dad. You were really lucky. That was such a close call," Leila said, bringing you over for him to hold.

Jerome kissed Leila on the forehead and took you into his arms. He gently rubbed the tip of his nose over your tiny little face and whispered incomprehensible sweet nothings into your ear.

I glanced over at the inTel as I folded a tea towel and noticed Governor Jacobson standing at a podium as if he was giving a speech.

"Abel, honey, can you turn that up?" I said. "Everyone, shh!"

We all turned our heads toward the inTel.

... Experts at the Neural Oscillation Registry have discovered an abundance of new sensory data collected

from a large sector of the population recently. This information has led us to initiate more research into the frequencies of oscillation that are linked to the perception and awareness of success. As a result, we have decided to reverse the new legislation until we know more. All letters of acceptance into a Transition Grave, and all scheduled death inducements, will be postponed until further notice. Everyone will receive notification from us explaining this in more detail. They will be mailed in the coming weeks ...

We stared in silence.

We had been a part of that population.

We had made a difference simply by asking questions and believing in ourselves—by trusting our instincts. You don't need an entire Globe of people violently revolting against the establishment to initiate change.

All it takes is one person—

to knock the first domino down.

WATCH AND LISTEN

So, that is everything you need to know, Eve. That's the end of my story. And please, *please*, don't worry. I will take very good care of you. DeathCare Therapists aren't like they used to be. And I'm an *especially* good one. 100% of my patients complete their therapy with a satisfied soul.

"I don't understand. Why am I here again?"

Eve, two years ago you suffered severe brain damage in a car accident, and you only have short-term memory and your hearing to rely on. As a result of this you have lost sight of your dreams and ambitions and time is running out for you. But I am determined to fix you. I *will* fix you. Even if you don't remember a single thing I've said by tomorrow, or the next day, or the day after that. This is the fourth time I've told you this story, Eve. Do you remember anything from the story I've just told you, Eve?

"Why aren't you DeathCare Therapists the way you used to be?"

Because now we all know, from *personal* experience, that you don't need your memory, nor do you need your career to be happy. Life is all about connecting with your true inner self, Eve. You just need to *believe*. Your heart is the organ that believes, Eve. It's your heart that knows it's never too late to feed your soul. Do you believe that, Eve?

You're frowning and spreading your fingers over your

knees just like your papou used to do.

"My grandfather?"

Yes. Jerome. From the story. Do you remember Jerome?

"When I entered the building, there was a bluebird singing next to me. Where did it come from?"

You're the first person to ever ask that question, Eve. I think we are going to get along very well here. That bluebird is happiness. Hold out two fingers and whistle for her. Go on, don't be shy. She'll perch on them."

"*Phwwwwwhht.*"

It needs to be a bit louder, Eve. It's okay. Let me show you. I'll whistle softly, but with certainty. Listen.

"Oh! Is that the bluebird?"

Yes, she's fluttering through the window now and she's landed on my two fingers.

The bluebird is facing me now. Listen to her whistle that sweet tune. I'm gently stroking her head. Come closer. Stroke her head, softly.

"She's so soft. She's beautiful."

"She's also very kind and very generous, and she always knows when you need her."

"How?"

"I can't tell you that yet. But keep trying to whistle for her, Eve. Wherever you are. If you do that, then one day she'll come ... without you whistling at all."

ACKNOWLEDGEMENTS

Thank you so much to the following people who made this book possible:

Musician, Anda Volley, for thinking of the music genre, PredaGroove, for the Ambriosial Inn scene with Jerome. Check out her music here: *andavolley.com*.

Writer, editor and longtime friend, Jenny Heath, for being the first to read the manuscript and boosting by ego by telling me it was the best book I'd ever written.

Editor and author, Dan Holloway, for doing the first manuscript evaluation when it was still very much in draft stage and rather embarrassing. He has a very kind and intellectual way of breaking bad news, leaving authors' egos intact.

Vine Leaves Press Publishing Director, Amie McCracken, for casting an eye over the manuscript before sending it off to my development editor and making me realize that my ambitious attempt at an omniscient point of view was just not working.

Vine Leaves Press development editor, Melissa Slayton, for helping me whip the 4th draft into a book I am super proud of. I couldn't have done it without her.

To the ladies in The Sanctuary group on Facebook who gave up their precious time to help me strengthen my book description.

And lastly, to all the people who assured me I would write again when I thought having a child would mean I'd never find the time. For the record, I still haven't found the time. The draft of this novel had been sitting on my hard drive since 2016, so all it needed was a keen eye and some revisions. Wish me luck for when I am next haunted by a blank page!

VINE LEAVES PRESS

Enjoyed this book?
Go to *vineleavespress.com* to find more.

www.ingramcontent.com/pod-product-compliance
Lightning Source LLC
Chambersburg PA
CBHW011747010726
47498CB00012B/2969